RL4   6.50

10

D1490950

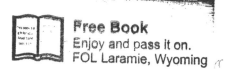

THE FINAL DECISION

THE FINAL DECISION

BARBARA NESBITT

Kids In Between, Inc.
409 Arbor Meadow
P.O. Box 1037
Ballwin, MO 63021
Phone: (314) 230-3887

Cover: Gail Schenk

ISBN:1-56734-034-2

DEDICATION

Thanks to Caren for her ideas and her friendship.

CHAPTER ONE

"You can come out now." Nina poked her head under the bed where Katie had hidden herself. "She's gone to work." Nina had stood at her bedroom door and waited until she heard her mother yell that she was leaving.

Katie rolled out from underneath the bed. "I always think that your mom must hear us talking or something." She stood up and stretched, wincing from the bruises and cut on her arm. "I just hate it when he uses that darn belt." Katie's fingers reached up to the most recent mark her father's temper had left on her.

"How long you going to stay this time?"

Katie shrugged. "Who knows. Maybe until tomorrow." She glanced down at the space under the bed where she had already hidden for two days. "My back is sore from laying still so much of the time. I sure wish your mom and dad would let you close your door."

"They could still come in here and catch us. Then I'd get it."

Katie sat down on the edge of the bed. "We're always getting it." She thought about the latest incident that had sent her running from the house to seek her hiding place in Nina's room. This time it was over bologna. Katie hated bologna, and that's what made it difficult to understand why her father thought she might have eaten the last of it. Bob Bennett had come into the kitchen and flung the refrigerator door open to get lunchmeat to fix himself a late night snack. It was after midnight when Katie heard him

1

scream out, "Where's the bologna? Who ate the bologna?"

Betsy, one of Katie's three sisters, turned and pulled the covers over her head. "Oh, God. He'll be in here in a minute and want to know which one of us ate the bologna."

Jane mumbled, "It wasn't me. I'm not taking the blame for it."

Katie glanced over at her youngest sister Melba who didn't say anything. "I bet it was Melba. Look at how she's pretending to be asleep. Melba, you're not sleeping. You heard dad. Did you eat the bologna?"

All of them were awake now. Each waited for their father to come through the door and shake them until one of them confessed that she had eaten all the lunchmeat. As they expected, Mr. Bennett threw open their bedroom door and yelled, "One of you brats doesn't have any consideration for the man of the house around here. Now which one of you got into that refrigerator just once too often? Which one of you didn't show respect for the breadwinner around here?"

Melba trembled awake and answered, "It wasn't me, Dad. I got a sick stomach and Mom just fixed me rice for supper. I couldn't eat any bologna. I was too sick."

The liar, Katie thought. Melba stuffed herself with meat and potatoes and cake at supper. "She's lying, Dad. She ate supper just like the rest of us."

Mr. Bennett walked over and pulled Katie out of bed. "You wouldn't be worrying about what Melba's got to say if you hadn't been the one wolfing down my bologna. Get

2

yourself in the other room." He pushed her along into the living room.

Katie took a deep sigh and tried to mentally prepare herself for the whipping that she was going to get. She was thinking how after the whipping, it would take her a long time to get to sleep. There was a test in algebra tomorrow, and algebra was her last class of the day. Being awake for so long meant that she would be tired and not do well on the test. She made one more effort to convince her father. "Dad, you got to know I hate bologna. I never eat bologna. When we have bologna for lunch, I always eat peanut butter. Don't you remember, Dad? I'm the one that hates bologna."

The noise and the yelling brought Katie's mother out of her bedroom. "What's going on out here?" It wasn't as if Lucy Bennett weren't used to the commotion brought on by her husband's anger, but she always felt some motherly need to make sure that he wasn't too hard on the girls and that the whippings weren't too severe. "What did she do now?"

"This one here ate my bologna. I was looking forward to a sandwich, and she polished off the last of the lunchmeat."

"Katie doesn't like bologna."

"What difference does that make? She ate it to spite me." He walked into the bedroom to get his belt.

Lucy shook her head at Katie. "You shouldn't have done that, Katie. You know how hard your father works to provide for us. The least we can do is see that he has a sandwich if he wants one."

Katie stood there waiting for her father to return. Arguing with her mother was pointless. In the end, she would side with him. Even if she didn't agree with him, she would never speak up or defy her husband. The best that Katie could say about her mother was that for almost a year she had kept some of what the girls and their brother did a secret. Rather than run to her husband to tell him what the children had done, she kept more things to herself now. As the children had grown older, Lucy seemed to get more weary of the endless arguments. This was particularly the case since her husband's temper had become worse over the years.

Lucy pulled at the belt on her robe. "Try to get some sleep after it's over." With that she turned and walked to her bedroom.

Katie had long ago quit asking how many times her father was going to whip her. Sometimes that made him angry and he would bellow out that maybe she needed one more for good measure.

When he reappeared, all Katie could think about was that she wished she *had* eaten the bologna. Somehow when she had done what he accused her of doing, it made it easier when the belt came down on her.

As he struck her, he always called out messages that he felt his children should hear. The message Katie hated the most was the one about his whipping her for her own good so that she could learn something. All that Katie learned on the night that the belt came down on her was that one way or the other, she was going to find out which of her sisters had eaten the bologna. Then she was going to hit her as hard as she could.

In the morning as she sat eating breakfast her father reached over and touched the marks that were already turning from a red to a light purple. "You wear something to cover up those arms. I don't want any of those snoops from school calling me about what's my business."

Katie moaned and looked up at the ceiling. "It's too hot to wear long sleeves."

Lucy set a box of cereal down on the table. "See, what you do, Katie, to get your father all riled up. You just can't ever do anything that you're asked to do." The last thing Lucy wanted was another call from the social worker who came twice a week to the school. Three months ago Mrs. Durbin had called to speak with Lucy. All her questions had to do with bruises that she had seen on the girls. Lucy had explained to Mrs. Durbin that the family had gone camping and fishing, and that the girls probably had gotten a little careless tramping around the woods. Lucy drilled that story into the heads of Jane and Katie so that their explanations to Mrs. Durbin would agree with what Lucy had told the social worker. From that time on, both Lucy and her husband made sure that whatever marks were left on the girls were carefully hidden by their clothing.

Katie sat quietly at the breakfast table trying to eat her

cereal. It seemed tasteless. Each bite was an effort to eat. She wasn't sure what was wrong, but she felt an overwhelming sense of sadness. She had studied hard for the algebra test and very much wanted to earn a good grade, yet she was already tired, and the test was five hours away.

Lucy glanced over at Katie. "What are you sitting there with that long face for? What if your face froze like that? You're not too pretty to start with. That's just what you need. A face with a frown that gets frozen on it. Isn't that right, Bob?"

"I just feel kind of down." Katie made another effort to spoon the cereal into her mouth.

"Down! You're not down. You're sitting in a chair like the rest of us. Eat that cereal and be glad there's food on the table. Plenty of kids go to school hungry. Why I know of families that don't even have a roof over their heads. You kids have always had the best because you've got a father that's such a hard worker. Now eat that cereal and quit your complaining."

Katie wanted to gag. "You know sometimes I think about killing myself." She hoped the words she spoke would make them take her seriously.

Lucy reached over and patted Katie on the shoulder. "Just be sure you do it in a room that doesn't have carpeting. Do it in the kitchen. Kitchen floors are easier to clean." Lucy dismissed what Katie said and turned to her husband. "Tonight's your bowling night, right?"

"Right. And when I get home and I want a bologna

sandwich, I expect to find bologna." He glared at Katie. "We got a house full of teenagers now and they don't seem to know any better than when they were toddlers." He stood up and put his cap on and was gone.

The girls all carried their plates to the sink. Lucy said, "It's Katie's turn to help get supper started tonight."

Betsy chimed in. "That's right. I helped last week."

"As sloppy and stupid as you are, Betsy, it wouldn't hurt you any to be helping every night. I swear. It's impossible to teach you anything."

Katie scraped her bowl clean and then rinsed it. "I'm not going to be here tonight. I'm running away again."

Jane laughed. "So who cares."

"I get her dessert." Bobbie called out from the door.

His late arrival to eat breakfast never bothered Lucy. If any of the girls had not been at the table when breakfast was ready, they would have been punished. Most of the time, though, Bobbie was able to do and say what he wanted without angering either his mother or his father. All of Bobbie's sisters had learned very early in life that both their parents would have preferred more sons and fewer daughters. By the time each had reached the age of two, they had a clear understanding that their lives would have been better if they had been boys.

Katie cracked a spoon against the sink. "I just don't understand how come no one cares when I run away? What kind of family is this, anyhow? One of the kids is missing and no one cares."

Lucy smacked Katie's hand. "Stop banging that silver-ware. You think money grows on trees and I can buy new silverware."

Katie came close to raising her voice, but she knew better. Yelling at her mother or defying her were two actions that Lucy still reported to her husband. "So why should I care or worry? You'll be back. You always come back."

"Well, suppose someday I don't. Suppose something terrible happens to me and I don't ever come back."

Lucy laughed. "Then Bobbie can have your dessert every night."

"And I can sleep in a bed by myself." Betsy danced around Katie. "I wish you would run away and not come back. I'm sick to death of sleeping with you. Mom, if Katie didn't come back, could I sleep in my own bed?"

Betsy's begging annoyed Lucy. Given how Lucy and her eight brothers and sisters were raised in a four room house by two alcoholic parents, Lucy firmly believed that her own children had a very good life. "You cut out that complaining, Betsy, or you'll find yourself sleeping on the floor. You kids just can't be grateful for anything."

"I was just asking." Betsy's lower lip dropped in a pout. "I'm not doing Katie's work if she runs away."

Lucy reached over and pinched Betsy's ear. "You'll do what your father and me tell you. That's what you'll do. Besides, we'll save some work for Katie. That is if she doesn't get murdered while she's gone. You want to be careful, Katie. If you tie up with a murderer, find yourself one that does in his victims real fast. You don't want to get tortured to death or anything like that. This family hasn't ever had anyone buried who had to have a closed casket."

Katie went back to her bedroom and slipped two changes of clothing into a paper bag. All she wanted this morning was that one of them would care that she was going to run away again.

The pattern for Katie's behavior had been set when she turned thirteen. Something would anger her parents. Then there would be the whipping. Katie would warn them that she was going to run away. Neither parent seemed to care. Her father's only comment was that there would be one less mouth to feed. Katie's mother gave her child some warning, like being careful that she didn't get hit by a truck or that she shouldn't fall down the stairs on her way out. All of her sisters argued about who would get Katie's possessions if she didn't come back. Bobbie's wants always revolved around getting Katie's share of the food.

Once Katie's warnings had been issued, and her parents and her brother and sisters had responded as they always did, Katie would take a few things with her and leave for some friend's house. At first her stays away from home were no more than overnight. By the time she was fourteen, Katie often was gone for three or four days. For the last six months Katie had been running to her friend Nina's house. Katie was never sure if her parents knew where she went. She was sure, though, that they didn't care that she was gone.

Katie's biggest problem when she stayed at Nina's was to keep herself hidden from Nina's parents. Months back they had discovered just how long Katie was staying. An overnight visit was fine, Nina's mother had said. Camping out and leeching off another family, as Nina's father described Katie's stay, was more than he wanted to put up with. After the first night of sleeping in Nina's room, Katie remained hidden. Long hours were spent under Nina's bed whenever Nina left the room for anything.

It was Bobbie who finally came by Nina's just to make sure that his sister actually was there. He stood in the doorway of Nina's room. Katie envied her brother so much. She knew that she was a better athlete than Bobbie could ever hope to be no matter how much he practiced. Her parents, though, never once came to see her play in the basketball tournaments or even to the championship baseball playoffs that Katie took part in. Neither parent had ever missed any game in which Bobbie played.

On weekends Mr. Bennett was out in the backyard throwing a basketball with Bobbie or playing catch with him. When Katie asked if she could play, her father would laugh and chase her away. "Go on, Katie. Get out of here. Girls can't play basketball. You in particular. You're too clumsy."

Katie kicked at the gravel along the edge of the driveway. "I made the A-team. That's better than Bobbie did."

"So who cares." Bobbie darted under the hoop and

dropped the basketball in. "Do like dad says. Get lost."

Out of all of them, though, it was only Bobbie who somehow seemed to know that there was an unfairness to the way the girls were treated. That's why he was the one who went in search of Katie when she was gone for what he thought was too long a period of time.

As Bobbie stood in the doorway of Nina's room, Katie looked at him and said what she always said when he came after her. "So what do you want?"

"Just checking on you." Bobbie moved inside the door.

"I haven't disappeared or anything if that's what you're thinking."

He laughed. "I knew that. I see you everyday at school. I didn't think you were dead or anything."

"Well, be sure and tell mom that the mass murderer and torturer didn't get me."

"You think you're funny, don't you. One of these days you are going to get in trouble if you don't quit this running away all the time."

"Like everyone says, who cares."

"You're right. Nobody does."

"So then why are you here?"

"Mom's fixing chili tonight. You really like chili."

"I suppose I do." Katie thought about her mother's chili. No matter what happened at home, Katie had to admit her mother was a very good cook. After four days at Nina's and eating nothing but the scraps of food Nina managed to save from her own meals, Katie believed that she was ready to go home. "Did they ask about me?"

"Not that I know about." Bobbie watched his sister stuff her belongings into the wrinkled bag. "You know how they are."

Katie wrapped her arms around the bag. "See you, Nina."

"Take care." Nina flopped down on her bed and waved. "See you at school in the morning."

The brother and sister walked along toward their house. Neither spoke. Katie wanted to ask what they all had been doing during the four days that she had been gone, but she knew Bobbie would shrug his shoulders and say they had not done anything. "What did she save for me to do?" Katie finally asked.

"The windows."

"All of them?" Katie made a face and shifted her bag.

"That's what she said. I heard her tell dad that Katie could just wash every window in the house."

"It's times like these that I'm sure glad we live in a small house."

Bobbie reached over and took the bag. "I'll carry it."

"Can I ask you something, Bobbie?"

"I don't care. But," he quickly added, "no one says I got to answer."

"What's it like sleeping in your own room? Like is it real quiet, or do you get lonely or what?"

"Quit asking stupid questions." He stepped up his pace and expected her to keep up.

When Katie entered the kitchen her mother stood stirring the chili. She turned and glanced at Katie. "Get the table set. Your father will be home in a few minutes. We got cornbread. Take a look at it in the oven and make sure it's not getting too brown."

"Bobbie said I got to do all the windows."

"That's right." Lucy wiped her hands on a dish towel. "Everyone around here carries their own load. You know it's not easy raising five kids. I wasn't in my right mind when I had all you kids. Now get the plates on the table."

Katie set the seven plates on the table, placing tablespoons and knives next to each plate. Years ago she had learned not to put forks on the table when her mother made chili. The lesson had been learned in one night. That was the night when she *had* put forks on the table. Her mother grabbed them up and gave Katie a shove.

"What's the matter with you? Don't you have a brain cell in your head? Now what is it you think we're going to eat with those forks?"

"I thought maybe..." The then ten-year-old Katie struggled for a reason why she might have put forks on the table just as she did every night.

"It doesn't pay for a stupid child to try and think. Now after dinner you're going to practice how to set a table when this family has chili."

Long after her brother and sisters sat watching television, Katie remained in the kitchen, setting the table over and over again. When it was time to go to bed, Katie cleared the table for the last time.

"Now you think you got it in that dumb little head of yours that there's a time for forks and there's a time when you don't need forks?"

A brief thought of the night she learned about forks flashed through Katie's mind as she now watched her mother pour the big pot of chili into a large mixing bowl and place it on the table. Lucy glanced at the kitchen clock. "Well, your father should be coming through that door just about now."

As she spoke the words, Bob Bennett walked into the kitchen. "Smells good." He nodded to his wife. Mr. Bennett sat down at the table. He looked at each of his children, his eyes finally resting on Katie. "You get to the windows first thing after school."

"Yes, Dad." Katie filled her large spoon with the chili that she loved. Washing the windows, she reasoned, was a fair punishment for running away. Though Katie hated the whippings, she always felt that whatever punishment they gave her, it was fair. Lucy and Bob Bennett, after all were her parents. They had to know, as they told her all the time, what was best for her.

Katie smiled at her mother. "You know what I was thinking about?"

Betsy rolled her eyes. "Now we got to hear what Katie's thinking."

"Let her speak." Lucy frowned at her oldest daughter. "We haven't heard anything out of her for four days."

14

It surprised Katie that her mother knew how long she had been gone. "I remembered how when I was learning to set the table and I put forks on when we had chili."

Lucy laughed. "See, Bob, it is possible to train a child. Even this here Katie can learn something. You hear that, Katie? I'm paying you a compliment even if you don't deserve it."

Katie returned the smile. "Thanks, Mom." Katie felt a rush of blood to her face as she blushed over what she took to be a genuine compliment from her mother. Maybe, Katie thought, if she tried harder, or was a little smarter, or could do things better she wouldn't be such a bother to her parents. Then sadly she stared down at her chili. She wondered why out of all of them, she was the least capable of doing anything right. After thinking for a few minutes about what a disappointment she must be to her mother and father, Katie said, "I'm going to clean those windows like you wouldn't believe. They're never going to be as clean as when I get done with them."

"Eat your chili," her father answered her. "And as for those windows, I'll believe it when I see it. You haven't done anything right around here in fourteen years. I sure don't see how as you'll start now."

Katie bent her head down and vowed that she would polish the windows until even her father would have to admit that they had never been cleaner.

CHAPTER TWO

For her fifteenth birthday, Katie decided she would leave the Churchill's and return home. Her absence this time had lasted for nearly three months, which was the longest Katie had ever been gone. When she asked Tania Churchill if she could come home with her, Katie didn't really know her all that well. The two of them had P.E. and English together. Other than seeing each other for their third and sixth hour classes, Katie shared little in common with Tania. All Katie knew was that the last incident with her father was enough to send her on yet another flight that took her away from home.

Katie had gone out with Blair. She hated his name, but she liked him because he was so good natured about most things. His easy-going manner was a welcome relief from the harshness of her own parents. Katie and Blair had gone to the show and later stopped for a hamburger. There was some doubt in Katie's mind as to whether or not there was time to eat and still be home by curfew. Enjoying Blair's company seemed to be more important than getting home at the exact time her father had told her to be home. It always puzzled Katie that she could be gone for days or for weeks and nothing was ever said about where she was. Yet, when she lived at home, if she arrived five minutes after her curfew, her father turned on her with an angry rage. His screaming always centered around her disobedience and lack of respect for him and her mother.

On the night when she and Blair arrived at her front

door, Katie was forty minutes late. The door flew open, and her father grabbed her arm. "The two of you get in here."

Katie cringed at the thought of Blair having to listen to her father lecture her. "It's not his fault, Dad."

"So he can't tell time, either?" Mr. Bennett stepped away from the door and motioned for them to follow him into the living room.

Blair shot Katie a glance. Then he shrugged his shoulders. He had never experienced anything like this on a date no matter how late he had brought the girl home. "I'm sure sorry, Mr. Bennett, if I upset you."

"Being sorry doesn't get it. Being home on time is what it's all about. Now I don't want you going out with my daughter again. Is that understood?"

"Yes, Sir." As Blair looked at the man's scowling face, about the last thing he wanted to do was take out Katie again.

Katie dropped her head down. Her eyes flitted upward so that she could see the expression on Blair's face. He looked frightened. "I told you, Dad, it wasn't Blair's fault. I know when I'm supposed to be home. We were just laughing and having a good time. We didn't know it was getting so late."

"Did I ask you for any kind of opinion?" He pointed his finger at Katie. "I'm talking to him, and I want him to understand I don't want him coming around here again. That's pretty simple."

17

"Dad, please. I really am sorry. It won't happen again. Will it, Blair?"

He knew it would not happen again because he had no intention of going near Katie. "It sure won't." Blair tried to edge his way toward the front door and away from the hard, mean look of Katie's father.

"Now are you going to shut up, Katie, or do I have to smack you?"

Katie bit her lip and fought back tears. "It's just that you keep..."

Her father's open hand hit against her cheek. "Stop getting me upset, Katie. I work hard all day. I don't want to be coming home to this."

Blair stood speechless as he looked at the red mark Katie's father had left on his daughter's face. "So long." He bolted for the door, tripping over an end table.

It was not getting yelled at that bothered Katie. That was a part of her life that she accepted. Nor was it getting slapped. Slaps and pushing and the whippings had been going on for as long as she could remember because of what she thought were the bad things that she did. What made her so angry was being hit in front of someone who was not a member of the family.

Katie went to bed knowing that in the morning she would have to make plans to run away again. On the way to school she decided she would ask Tania Churchill for help.

Before gym class started, Katie approached Tania. "I

think you live about six blocks from me. Am I right or wrong?"

"Huh?" Tania bent down to tie her shoes.

"Do you think I could come and stay at your house for awhile?"

A puzzled look crossed Tania's face. "Are you kidding me or what?"

"Oh, no," Katie answered. "I need some place to stay for say..." Katie stopped to think how long she should be gone. "I guess maybe a month."

"Why?"

"Things are terrible at home. I got to get away for awhile. I do that all the time. My friend Nina can't let me stay anymore. Sometimes I used to stay at Leslie's, but she moved. You remember Leslie. That tall blond girl with the accent. She was from Germany."

"I don't think you can stay at my house. There are six of us. My dad's dead. We don't have much room." Tania wasn't sure why she felt sorry for the girl whom she barely knew. "It's so crowded at our place you got to go outside to change your mind."

"I heard that one. We say it at our place, too." Katie smiled slightly to show that she wasn't being too critical of Tania. "I don't mind being crowded. I'm used to it. I can be a big help. I know how to cook and clean. My mother taught me how to clean really good." Katie moved closer to Tania and looked directly into her eyes. "Let me try and talk to your mom. I bet you I can convince her to let me stay."

"What makes you so sure that *I* want you to stay? I hardly know you."

"I'll do all your work for you. You can just sit and watch television and I'll do whatever your mother makes you do. Is it a deal?"

"Let me think about it. I'll let you know sixth hour."

At the end of sixth hour Katie hurried to catch up with Tania. "So what do you think?"

"I guess it doesn't matter, but remember, you're the one who has to talk my mother into it."

"Right after school I'll start working on her."

"Not hardly. She doesn't get home from work until six."

At the end of the school day Katie tugged on Tania's arm. "Come on. We'll head over to my house and I'll get my stuff."

Tania yanked her arm free. "Wait a minute. No one even said you could stay."

"Don't worry about it. It's a sure thing." Katie had dealt with so many mothers other than her own that dealing with one more didn't concern her. She never doubted for a minute that she would be able to talk Tania's mother into allowing her to stay.

Very quickly Katie grabbed her clothes off the hooks on the wall. "About the only time my sisters don't try and sell my clothes is when I'm home. Can you imagine, Tania, here I was walking down Federal Boulevard and I see this girl. She's got on one of my sweaters and one of my skirts. I stopped her and asked her where she got those clothes. She said she bought them. I knew right then and there that Jane sold my clothes to that stupid girl. Jane just has no idea about property and who owns it. She sees something that isn't hers, and it might as well be because she takes it, anyhow."

"So did you get your sweater and skirt back?"

"Heck no." Katie folded up her three sweatshirts. "What was I supposed to do? Demand that this strange girl take off my clothes? Besides, how would she have known she bought the stuff from my thieving sister."

"Don't you get tired of all your brothers and sisters?"

"I only got one brother. He's at least better than my sisters."

Tania picked up a nail file and cleaned her nails while she waited for Katie to finish gathering up her things. "You know what I dream about?"

"What?"

"Taking a long bath without someone pounding on the door and yelling that they want to get in or that they got to use the toilet."

"Yeah. I know what you mean. Most of the time one of my sisters is in the bathroom telling me what's wrong with my body or my face. Betsy's got this really great figure, and she sure makes a point of making me miserable about mine. Do you get along with your family?"

Tania made a face. "Naw. I hate them all. Well," she

sort of pouted, "I guess I don't hate them. I just don't have much to say to them. You'll have to sleep with me and my sisters."

Katie grinned. "Just like home." She put the last of her belongings in the bag. "Let's go."

"Aren't you going to leave a note or nothing?"

"They'll figure it out when I'm not home for dinner."

Tania walked in front of Katie as they closed the door behind them. "I can't believe this. Why my mother would have the cops all over the place if I was twenty minutes late for dinner. And here you're trying to tell me that your parents don't even care that you're gone. I never heard of such a thing."

Katie waved her finger at Tania. "You sure said the right words. *They don't care.* They really don't." It made Katie sad to say what she knew to be true. "I guess maybe they got so many kids that one of them being gone doesn't matter. My brother Bobbie is the pet. I guess because Melba is the youngest she gets some special treatment. Isn't *Melba* a dumb name?"

"It sounds like the name of a cookie." Tania slowed down her pace so that Katie could keep up.

Katie laughed. "It's funny you should say that. There actually is some kind of melba toast. Mom told me that. Anyhow, Melba never seems to get in much trouble. Dad mainly gets after me, Jane, and Betsy. Me especially. But then I suppose it's because I'm not very likeable and I'm always doing stuff I'm not supposed to do."

22

"Like what?"

"Oh, I don't know." Katie didn't know where to begin because there were so many things that she did every single day of her life that somehow upset her parents. "Like I forget to put the milk on the table, or I leave a window open and it rains. Stuff like that."

"That's nothing."

"Yeah it is. I'm just stupid."

"You don't seem stupid."

"Well, I am." Katie felt she had no choice but to believe what her mother and father told her.

Tania pointed up the walk to a small frame house. "This is it."

The small white bungalow was much like Katie's own house in size, though Tania's house was badly in need of paint. The yard was littered with paper and toys. One of the windows was covered with cardboard, and the front door didn't close properly.

Katie found the messy house in sharp contrast to the cleanliness and neatness that Lucy and Bob demanded. "It's kind of a mess."

"You think the outside is bad, wait until you see the inside."

Tania was right. Once inside, Katie was shocked at the clothes piled on the floor and at the food and dirty dishes that lay scattered around the floor. "Don't you guys ever clean this place?"

"Not if we can help it." Tania took off her sweater and

dropped it on a chair. "It's home sweet home to us."

A tall, nice looking boy came from the kitchen. He was eating a piece of pizza. "So what's going on?" He eyed Katie.

"What's ever going on in my life?" Tania kicked her shoes into a corner. "This is my friend. She's Katie. Katie, meet my brother, the slob."

"Look who's talking, Miss Piggy." He swept some clothes to the floor and sat down in a chair. "I'm Gary."

"I'm Katie Bennett."

"So Tania said. You live around here?"

"About six blocks away. I'm going to see if your mom will let me stay here." As Katie glanced at the nasty living room, she wondered if it were possible to live like this.

"Oh, man. That's what we need around here is another warm body. Are you nuts, Tania or what?"

"Nothing is for sure yet." Tania walked into the kitchen to get her own slice of pizza. "Mom doesn't know about it or anything. Me and Katie were just talking. It was her idea."

Gary slumped down even farther in the chair, stretching out his legs. "So how come you got this idea? You running away or something?"

Katie cleared away a dirty plate from the couch and sat down. "I always run away. I do it when things get sort of impossible at home. My parents really don't care."

"Cool. Real cool." Gary grinned. "I keep thinking about taking off myself. I want to head for Canada."

24

"Canada!" Katie's mouth fell open. "That's another country. Why would you want to go to another country?"

"For the adventure. Besides, mom would have a harder time bringing me back. She wouldn't think of looking for me in Canada."

Tania took a bite of the pizza and frowned. "Gary here is mom's problem child. She doesn't even know he quit school and works at this gas station. She's going to kill him when she finds out. Gary, you're just always causing trouble. You need to grow up and get a brain."

Gary sat up straight and glared at his sister. "And since when did you start growing wings and get a halo? You should see some of the stuff she pulls what with her stealing and all. Mom would be a lot less upset to find out I quit school than she would be if she found out about you and your stealing."

Tania shot a quick glance at Katie. At the moment, Tania hated her brother for telling on her. "He's a liar."

Katie shrugged her shoulders. "Don't look at me. I don't care. I steal stuff myself."

Gary stood up and paced back and forth. "So now we got another thief in the house. I better nail down everything I own."

Katie tried to be humorous when she said, "I think if you just wait awhile, it will rot away in this place."

Gary didn't think her remark was funny. "Listen, don't be knocking this place. If your own home is so great, just haul your butt back to it."

Tania thumped her finger against Katie's face. "Come on you two. Cut it out. Hey, look at the time. It's nearly five-thirty. Mom's going to be home before long."

"So." Gary returned to his slumping position.

"So." Tania angrily looked at the brother for whom she had little use. "Katie said she was going to fix supper and surprise mom. That's what."

"Surprise her! Having supper on the table would plain cause her to have a stroke. You see," Gary turned to look at Katie, "the aim of this family is to do as little as possible. Our motto is why work when you can sit and do nothing."

"That's your motto, Slimeball. Not mine." Tania stared at him in disgust.

"Listen, I work. What are you talking about? You and those lazy sisters and brother of mine are the ones who come home and plant your butts in front of the television and do nothing. You don't even care that mom works all day to feed you slobs."

Katie stood up. Their arguing annoyed her. "Let's just get supper ready."

"Who's us?" Gary asked.

Katie shrugged. "I guess me."

"That's more like it."

When Ann Churchill came through the kitchen door, her mouth fell open. The dirty dishes had been cleaned out of the sink, the table was set, and a mound of spaghetti sat in the middle of the table. "What's this?" She put her hand to her mouth. "Someone actually cooked dinner. Has my

26

family gone crazy!"

"Mom," Tania motioned her arm toward Katie. "This is my friend Katie. She did it."

"Well, I certainly do thank you." Ann took off her coat. She continued to look around the kitchen in disbelief. "I don't got no idea who you are, Katie, but I sure thank you for fixing dinner."

"You're welcome, Ma'am." Katie felt very pleased with herself. She felt confident that by the time she had washed and dried the dishes and cleaned off months of dirt and grease from the stove, she would be more than welcome in the Churchill home.

The conversation at the dinner table was much like the ones that took place at Katie's own home. The only difference was that Ann Churchill remained totally silent as her children argued back and forth about nothing of importance. Katie took almost no part in the conversation. She simply sat and listened, feeling sorry for the mother who looked more than tired.

When the meal was over, Katie insisted that Ann go sit in the living room. "I'm telling you I can clean up. I really don't mind."

Ann stared at Katie. "Why you're a stranger. There's no call for you to be cleaning up after all these slobs."

Katie put her hands on the back of Ann's shoulders. "Please. Just don't worry about it. I'm going to take care of it." A smile spread across Katie's face. She was sure that she had won Ann Churchill over.

27

From the kitchen Katie could hear them arguing about what they would watch on television. Gary being the oldest and the strongest, wrestled the remote control free from his sister Georgia. Whether they liked it or not, all of them watched what Gary wanted to watch.

An hour later when Katie came out of the kitchen, she tapped Ann on the shoulder. "Do you want to see what I did?"

Immediately Ann pushed herself out of the chair. "Why that's the least I can do." Ann followed Katie into the kitchen, trailed by Tania. Once again Ann stood and looked in amazement. "This has got to be the cleanest this kitchen has been since we moved in. You certainly must come from a home where proper training was given." Ann brushed a wisp of hair from her forehead. "I sure do wish I could have gotten my kids to do a little helping around the house."

"Thank you, Ma'am." Katie rushed over to fold a dish towel that she had forgotten about. "I really like cleaning and working." She glanced over at Tania and signaled her to say something.

"Mom," Tania walked to where her mother stood. "Katie here needs a place to stay. We were sort of thinking that she could stay with us."

"You what?" Ann turned to face her daughter. "Stay here! Why we're wall to wall with kids now. What on earth am I going to do with another one?"

"You saw how clean Katie is." Tania's voice took on a

28

tone of pleading. "Katie's folk have been real mean to her. She just had to leave or else they were going to kill her. She can do all kinds of things to help you, Mom. Come on, Mom, don't say no before you even think about it?"

"Is that true, Katie? Are your parents out to harm you?"

Katie never thought that her parents meant her any harm, but she lied, anyhow. "Oh, yes, Mrs. Churchill. My father has told me all kinds of times that he's going to kill me. I had to get out to save my life. And," Katie quickly added, "it is like Tania says. I will earn my way around here."

"What about the police? I don't want to get in any kind of trouble."

"Believe me," Katie assured her, "my parents don't care if I'm gone." Katie felt confident that she was now telling the truth. "The police won't come here if that's what you're thinking."

Ann sat down on a wobbly kitchen chair. "I just don't know. Where will she sleep?"

Tania grinned. If her mother were asking such questions, it was just a matter of keeping after her until she broke down and consented. "In my room on the floor. We got some extra quilts and stuff."

"Yeah." Katie smiled at Mrs. Churchill. "I'm used to sleeping on the floor. And," Katie knelt down to look at the chair where Mrs. Churchill sat, "I can fix that chair. I'm real handy. You got some glue and some string. I'll fix that chair right now."

It was mainly Katie's eagerness to please that finally won over Ann Churchill. Within a week, Ann didn't know how their family could exist without the young girl. The entire house was cleaned and meals were on the table every night when Ann walked through the door. No matter what Katie said to Tania's brothers and sisters about picking up their own clothes and half-eaten food, none of them made an effort to help her. Katie took to scooping up their clothes and stuffing them in a closet. She warned them that if their clothes were not hung up and sorted out, they would not be washed. Her warning went unnoticed. Each of them wore clothes that were wrinkled or dirty rather than make the effort to take them to the basement where Katie could wash them.

It was the horrible habits of the Churchill family rather than missing her own family that finally drove Katie to leave. Katie's hope had been that Tania and her brothers and sisters would change if they were shown how neat and tidy the house could be, but as Katie came to realize, all of them didn't really care how they lived. As Katie's fifteenth birthday neared, she knew that she would go home once again. Only Ann and Tania protested. Tania had grown to like Katie, and Ann had come to depend on her.

"You're a very good girl, Katie." Mrs. Churchill's eyes filled with tears as she watched Katie gather up her things. "I just can't believe that your family hasn't missed you."

"They'd never say so even if they did." Katie accepted

what she knew to be true. "They knew I was here and they never once came over and asked me to come home."

Tania frowned. "Then why you leaving?"

"I've run away long enough. Maybe things will be different. Besides, it's report card time. I'll need my parents to sign my card. And," Katie broke out with a grin, "it's my birthday tomorrow."

It was still difficult for Tania to understand the relationship Katie had with her family. "Listen, if they don't care nothing about you running away all the time, what makes your birthday so important?"

"They'll have a cake. They always have a cake and a present for all of us. That's an important tradition in our family. I guess it sort of shows that they did want us to be born even if they tell us something else." Katie thought about how many times her mother had told her that she wished none of them had ever been born. The birthday cakes and the presents, though, made Katie believe that her mother didn't mean it when she said how happy her life would have been if she hadn't had so many children.

On her last night at the Churchill house, Gary made a generous gesture. Over the protests of his brothers and sisters, he handed the remote to Katie. "It's your choice tonight."

Katie smiled and thanked him.

As the time moved closer to midnight, all the children began drifting off to the two bedrooms where they shuffled about looking for a space to sleep. Even in their sleeping

31

habits, there was no order to their lives. Gary remained behind. He reached out and took Katie's hand. Then he turned around and put his arms around her.

Katie cringed and pulled away. Katie was not used to being touched by anyone. She could not remember either her mother or father ever hugging her or touching her with affection. "Don't be doing that. You got no business touching me or anything."

"I kind of like you, Katie."

"Sure. You like me because I pick up your sloppy messes and wash your socks."

"I'd like you even if you left my stinky socks all over the floor."

"Well, I don't like you." Katie wasn't sure if she had told him the truth. There was something about Gary that set him aside from the rest of Tania's family. Perhaps it was the fact that he left the house everyday and went to work.

Gary let his hands drop to his side. "If you ever decide you want to run away to Canada, let me know."

"That will be the day."

Instead of going to the Churchill house after school, Katie headed up the street toward her own home. As she entered the living room, Katie realized that it had been such a long time since she had seen the familiar things in her life. Nothing looked different. After months at the Churchill's, the cleanliness of her own home surprised her. Katie had almost forgotten what it was like to live the way her family lived. Suddenly it struck Katie what good parents she really must have. Despite the fact that seven of them crowded together in the small house, everything was neat and tidy. Katie could not help but compare her own training and her own abilities with how little Tania's brothers and sisters knew how to do.

Katie heard her mother rattling dishes in the kitchen. She called out, "I'm back." Katie walked into the kitchen and half waved at her mother. "Are we going to have a cake tonight?"

Lucy didn't even turn around to look at Katie. "Have we ever missed anyone's birthday around here?"

"I don't think so."

"What do you mean you don't think so? Have we or haven't we?"

"Yeah, Mom. We've always had a cake and a present for everyone's birthday."

"That's more like it."

"Mom," Katie moved closer to where her mother was wiping down the refrigerator. "I want to thank you."

"For what?"

"For teaching me so much stuff. I mean I really know a lot about keeping house and cooking and all kinds of stuff. You should see how those Churchills live. They're real pigs. The girls can't do anything."

"I don't want to be hearing about the Churchills. Your brother said they were trash. Now that you've had your fill of trash, you've come home to see how decent folks live."

"Is it a chocolate or white cake?"

"Your favorite is chocolate."

"Then it's chocolate?" Katie smiled at her.

Lucy turned around and put her hand on her hip. "And why would we want to get your favorite when we could get you one you didn't like?"

A look of disappointment crossed Katie's face. "Then it's not chocolate?"

"Oh, for heaven sakes. You just take everything so seriously. You can't even joke with you."

One of the biggest problems Katie had in understanding her parents was in trying to figure out when they were serious and when they weren't. A dozen times a week Katie heard them say that she took things too seriously, but her mother's remarks always sounded serious to Katie.

"Sometimes you joke, Mom, and sometimes you seem like you mean what you say. I don't always know. Like when I told you I was going to drown myself, you told me not to get any water on the floor because I'd ruin the tile. I don't know if you were kidding or not."

"See." Lucy looked disgusted with Katie. "What mother would want her kid to actually drown herself?"

"Maybe some mothers would."

"Well, I'm not one of them. You're just stupid how you think your father and me mean everything we say."

"Okay, then. I'll try to do better and not take every-thing so seriously." Their discussion made Katie feel as if she had never left home. It was as if the things they talked

34

about were the same things she talked about before she left. Nothing, Katie, reasoned was ever settled.

"Get yourself cleaned up for dinner. You probably still got dirt on you from that sty you chose to stay at."

"Maybe I'll take a bath."

Lucy grinned, "And if you decide to drown yourself because we got you a white cake, don't get any water on the floor." Lucy turned back to finish cleaning the refrigerator.

CHAPTER THREE

Rod Powalkski sat next to Katie in her homeroom. No matter how many times she dropped her books on the floor, he never bent down to pick them up, which was a sure sign to Katie that he didn't like her. Tania kept insisting that Katie ask him to the school's Valentine Day's dance, but Katie didn't feel good enough about herself to deal with what she would do if he turned her down.

Tania took it upon herself to ask Rod if he wanted to take Katie. That he did, astounded Katie. In homeroom she whispered to him, "Is what Tania said true?"

He barely smiled. "About the dance?"

Katie nodded and waited for his reply.

"Yeah. I'll go with you."

"Go with me or take me? There's a difference."

"What's the difference?" A lock of his brown hair fell down on his forehead.

"If you take me you have to pick me up."

"I don't mind picking you up."

"I'd rather you just went with me. That way I can meet you at the dance." Katie remembered what had happened on her last date with Blair. She had no intention of repeating that evening.

"No problem. I'll just meet you there."

"Are you getting all dressed up?"

"Probably not." Rod looked down at his worn jeans. He had no clothes that would qualify for dressed up. "I'll probably wear what I got on or something just like them."

"That's okay." Katie opened her book. "I'll see you there." She made a few notes in an effort to outline the chapter. Then she leaned over and whispered, "Are you going to be there when it first starts?"

"You want me there then?"

"I can get some booze if you want to meet me earlier."

"I don't drink." Rod looked at her strangely. "Do you?"

Katie chose not to answer truthfully. "Oh, no." In the last few months her weekends were filled with drinking the liquor that she stole from grocery stores. Before she lived with the Churchill family, Katie had stolen only clothes. Gary had introduced her to liquor. Although Katie hated the taste of whiskey, she came to like the uncaring, easy going way life felt after drinking. Two or three afternoons a week when Gary would get home from work early, the two of them would sit and watch television and drink together. After leaving the Churchills, Katie found that it seemed easier to ignore some of what her parents said and did if she took a few drinks after school.

As she bent over her books in homeroom, she now and then glanced over at Rod. He had made it clear that he didn't drink. Katie decided she would do her drinking before she met him at the dance. Other than knowing that he didn't drink, Katie knew very little about Rod. He was not popular at school, which is why Katie thought he might take her out. The prettier girls who belonged to the clubs and who were cheerleaders dated the best looking boys.

Katie did not think of herself as being the least attractive. It would never have occurred to her that any of the good looking boys would ask her out. In a way, she realized she was settling for far less than the best when she let it be known that she wanted to go to the dance with Rod.

Another thing that Katie knew about Rod was that he worked after school. Because he worked, Katie wondered why he dressed so shabbily. He never wore new clothes, and all of his shirts looked as if they had been purchased at a bargain store. They were short-sleeved shirts. And they were that common plaid that only the poor students wore. As she glanced over at his old and dirty tennis shoes, she wondered if he would embarrass her at the dance. Katie decided that she would steal a new shirt for him.

Near the end of the homeroom period the teacher called each of their names, and each student received a grade slip. As Katie took hers, the teacher commented, "You did a good job this semester."

Katie reached for the yellow slip. "Gosh! Three A's. I wasn't expecting that. I can't believe I got an A in geometry."

"Mrs. Bannion said you aced the final. Good work."

All through dinner Katie was anxious for the meal to end so that she could show her parents her grade slip. When the dishes were cleared away and her father planted in his favorite chair, Katie approached him. "I got my grade slip today. I did really good."

He held up the newspaper and turned the page. "Is that

a fact. Katie, while you're standing there will you put on the news?"

Katie walked over and changed the channel. "Do you want to see my grades?" She reached in her pocket and took out the yellow slip. "I got an A in geometry."

Bob Bennett shook his head and looked over at Lucy. "What kind of standards do you think these schools must have now? Giving a kid like her an A in geometry. When I went to school you really had to work for an A. Now they just hand them out like they were lima beans or something."

"Let me see, Katie." Lucy reached over and took the grade slip. "She's right. She did get an A in geometry. One in English and one in science. What do you think about that, Bob?"

"What else did she get?" He went right on reading his paper.

"She got a B in geography and a C in social studies."

"And, young lady, why didn't you get A's in everything?"

Katie blushed. "We were supposed to draw this map of Asia and label all the countries. I didn't know it was supposed to include South Asia. I left off all the South Asian countries. That really took me down in geography."

"You probably weren't listening. That's how you do around here. You can't get anything straight. If there's a way to screw something up, you'll sure figure out how to do it."

Katie watched her mother scribble her name on the grade slip that had to be returned. "I've got to get my grades up if I hope to go to college."

"College!" Her father dropped his paper into his lap. "Now, Lucy, isn't that something. This empty head talking about college. And just where do you think we're going to get money to send you to college? If anyone goes to college it will be Bobbie and not some girl."

Katie was not to be put off. "I can work and maybe get a scholarship or something."

Her father banged his fist on the arm of the chair. "Oh, Lord. A scholarship. You don't even vacuum right and here you are talking about a scholarship. You'll be lucky to get a job mopping floors let alone getting any scholarship." He leaned over and commented to Lucy, "Where do these stupid kids get these ideas?"

"If I can get a scholarship, would you let me go to college?"

"Shut up about this college stuff. You can go out and work just like I did. You kids today got it too easy. You know what my life was like. Well, I'm going to tell you. It was hell. Beatings everyday by two drunks. Work until you drop. They hauled us out of school the day we turned sixteen and put us to work, and I been working everyday since. If we opened our mouths to talk about some dumb thing like college, we'd have gotten our teeth knocked out. Kids knew their place back then. If we didn't, there was always someone to cuff us up the side of the head and

40

remind us that we were nothing and we better shut up. Isn't that right, Lucy?"

Lucy handed the signed grade slip back to Katie. "Your dad's right. We never thought about college in our house. In fact, we never thought about much of anything. I was one of the lucky ones because I was able to finish high school. Just getting through high school, Katie, that's enough for you. You don't need to be making any grand plans about your life. Now me and your father, we know about those things. I didn't have it any easier than he had it. Why if I didn't do something right, my father laid it to me. He made a believer out of me. That mother of mine what with being drunk all the time, never had a kind word to say to any of us. You can thank your lucky stars that you didn't grow up in a home like I had. You can't believe how happy I was when your father came along and wanted to marry me. It was the happiest day of my life when I left that no-good mother of mine and that mean father.

"That's what you ought to be thinking about for your future. Finding a good, hard worker like your father. You're not going to find that kind of man at college. You get yourself through high school. Then get yourself a good husband." Lucy waved her finger at Katie. "But I'll tell you something, though, don't be having a bunch of kids. They take it all out of you."

Bob looked sternly at Katie. "Especially this one. We could have done without this one."

Katie looked away. "When you say things like that,

you hurt my feelings."

Bob shook his head and pulled the newspaper up in front of his face. "You're just too sensitive, Katie. You need to toughen up or the world is going to walk all over you."

"Would you like it if I kept telling you that you were a pain in the butt and I wished you'd never been born? Well, would you?"

"Listen here, young lady." He reached over and shook Katie. "Don't you be putting me through any third degree about what I'd like and not like. Now if you don't shut up, I'm going to smack you one."

Katie put her grade slip back in her pocket and asked to be excused.

"Fine," her father answered. "It will be a welcome relief to get you out of here and get some peace and quiet."

Lucy rose and followed Katie to her room. "As for me, Katie, I think you did pretty good at school." This was as close to a compliment as Lucy was capable of giving her daughter. "What your father and me are trying to tell you is that it's a hard world. Your dad and me learned that when we were kids. That's all we want is for you children to be able to survive without getting hurt all the time. You got to agree, Katie, you are awful sensitive."

Katie pushed Betsy's clothes off the bed and onto the floor. "I just wish you guys wouldn't always be telling me..."

Lucy put her hand over Katie's mouth. "That's what

your father was saying, Katie. We don't want to be hearing about what your wishes are. Now get this room cleaned up, and don't be throwing your sister's clothes on the floor." Lucy stepped to the door. On the hook above the door was a new raincoat. "Is this new?"

"Yeah." Katie nodded.

Lucy looked at the brandname. "That's an expensive coat. I recognize the label. I've seen those advertisements. Where did you get it?"

Katie's fists doubled up and she felt her pulse increase. "I stole it."

"Stole it and didn't get caught?" Lucy's eyes widened.

"That's right."

"Well, I'll be. I'll have to let your father know that at least there seems to be one thing you can do right."

Katie let out a deep sigh. She wasn't sure why she knew that if she told her mother the truth about the raincoat, that Lucy wouldn't care. Katie lay down on the bed for a few minutes of quiet before her sisters came home. She couldn't help but wonder why her mother became so upset if she would find a strand of hair in the sink after Katie had cleaned the bathroom, and yet, she seemed to feel some pride in Katie being successful at stealing a raincoat.

Worn out from listening to their stories about their own miserable childhoods, and disappointed at having to accept that she would never go to college, Katie did what she had been doing more and more lately. She reached under the bed and took out the cardboard box that contained her socks and underwear. Beneath her personal belongings was the liquor that she was coming to depend on more and more to make her feel better. Katie brought the bottle to her lips and drank down two gulps. Then she took out the toothpaste that she also kept hidden in the box. She spread the paste on her finger and vigorously rubbed her teeth and gums to take away the smell of the whiskey. She dozed off thinking about the Valentine's Day dance.

On the night of the dance, Katie wrapped the sweater that she had stolen for Rod in a brown paper bag. It was an expensive, argyle sweater. A bottle of rum also was in the bag. When she arrived at the dance, she violated the rules by going to her locker to hide the sweater and the liquor, but not before she had taken several swallows and rubbed her teeth with the toothpaste that she carried in her jeans.

Rod waited just inside the door of the gym. He smiled when he saw her. "You look nice. Is that a new sweater?"

"Real new." Katie had just stolen it that very afternoon. "My sister will have it sold by Monday."

Katie looked at him and wished that she could return the compliment about his looking nice. He didn't. He wore the same jeans that had not been in fashion for several years. He had on the same red plaid shirt with its frayed sleeves that he usually wore to school.

"I can see you made a real effort to get yourself all dressed up."

"I told you I don't have any new clothes." He blushed when he tried to defend himself.

"Where do you get your clothes? The Salvation Army or something."

"As a matter of fact, I do." There was no apology for what he said. "My mom does the best she can with what she's got, and that's not much."

"Tell me something I don't know." Katie realized when she insulted him that she was getting more like her parents all the time.

"You sure know how to insult a guy."

"So. I get insulted all the time. It toughens you up."

"Where did you learn that?" He thought about the gentleness of his own mother and what she taught him.

"My mom and dad." Katie had come to believe that her parents had to be right because they repeated the same things so often that what they said must be true.

"My mom says there's too much cruelty in the world as it is. Like she says, you can't go wrong if you treat people with kindness. I get the idea that you're not a real kind person."

"Why do you say that?" Katie certainly never thought of herself as mean.

"I hear you talking at school. You cut people down. You really know how to get to them."

"I'm just being funny."

"Do you hear them laughing?" He moved along beside her toward the soda on the tables near the back of the gym.

"They're too sensitive." Katie defended herself with the same argument her mother and father used.

"Maybe you're too tough on them. That's probably why you don't have too many friends."

"Now hold on." Katie turned on him. "Who says I don't have many friends?"

"I never see you with anyone except Tania."

"And you got this big following or what? No one has anything to do with you because you dress like a rag picker and you're always studying."

"I can't help it because I come from a poor family. My dad died about five years ago. It's just me and mom and my brother. One of these days I'm going to get a college education and take care of her."

Katie laughed out loud. "You! Get a college education. You got to be kidding. You need to get yourself a few new shirts before you start thinking about going to college."

"See. That's what I mean. You just cut me down."

"I told you. Toughen up." Katie waved to a girl across the room. "There, Mr. Know-It-All. I know people." Katie made a point of waving to a boy in her geometry class. "That guy Wilson is always copying off my paper. I told him he's dumber than a piece of string and ought to be in basic math."

"Yeah. I bet you did. Do you want to dance?"

"I don't like to dance."

"Why?"

"Because I don't like anyone holding or touching me."

Rod glanced over at her. "How come?"

"That's the way I am. Take it or leave it."

"Then why did you have Tania ask me if I wanted to take you to the dance?"

"I wanted a date for the dance. I guess I just wanted to get out to one of these big social events. You got a problem with that?"

"Sure beats me why you'd go to all that trouble."

"Let's go outside. I got something for you."

"What?"

"You'll see. Follow me." Katie wound her way through the crowd and to the hall where her locker was located. "Wait here."

"We're not supposed to go to our lockers."

"So have me arrested." Katie ran down the hall to her locker and turned the combination. She took the sweater out of the bag and ran back to where Rod waited.

"What's that?"

"A new sweater for you. I got it especially for you."

Rod looked at the sweater that he was sure must have cost her fifty dollars. "I can't take anything like that from you. Why did you go and spend all that money on me? You barely know me."

Katie laughed. "I didn't spend a dime on it if you know what I mean."

"You mean you stole it?" He backed away from her "You're a shoplifter!"

"It's something I do very good." Katie tried to hold the sweater up against him. "Look. It fits."

47

Rod looked at her in amazement. "I'm not wearing anything that's stolen."

"If I was you, Rod, I'd wear anything I could get except what you have on."

"You know what I think, Katie?"

"What?"

"The next time you want a date for a dance, you ask some fool. I'm not a fool. I'm not a thief, and I don't down booze."

"You're perfect then. I end up with a perfect date except he's dressed like a country bumpkin. You got some nerve, Rod, judging me. You're just this jerk. If I hadn't asked you to this dance, you can bet your life every girl in this school would have turned you down."

"You're probably right. And you know something else? More than anything, I wish you'd turned me down." He stalked off down the hall and disappeared out the front door.

Katie made a trip back to the gym to find Tania. She was on the dance floor with Nate Collier. Katie waved for Tania to come over, but Tania shook her head and went on dancing. As she saw Tania move about the floor with Nate, Katie wondered what it would be like to have someone's arms around her. When the dance finally ended, Katie went to the edge of the floor and grabbed Tania's arm.

"What a wasted evening. That dumb Polack doesn't know anything. He doesn't drink. He wouldn't take the sweater I got for him. He couldn't understand why I don't like dancing. I might as well have stayed home."

Tania threw her hands up in the air. "Me now. I'm having a great time. Nate wants to know if I want to go steady. What do you think, Katie?"

"Do you think I care about Nate. I got my own problems. Do you want to go outside? I got a bottle in my locker."

"No way. In fact I got to get back to Nate. Is he ever something else. I wonder where he's been all my life."

"In a rathole."

"Katie! Why do you say such terrible things? He's real nice and he's a great dancer."

"Well, if you really like him, keep him away from your oink-oink family."

Tania looked hurt at what Katie said. "They were good enough for you when you didn't have any place else to go."

"Had I known about any other place, I would have went there. I still have to take two baths a day to get the Churchill stench off me."

"I don't need friends like you." Tania turned her back on Katie and walked away.

The night air was almost too frigid for Katie to stand outside for very long. She pulled her coat collar up and started for home. Katie took the shortcut through the park. On the path that led to the street where she would turn to go home, Katie sat down on a bench. She pulled out the bottle of rum and gulped some down. The heat of the liquor made her body and mind feel better. With each gulp it

49

seemed less important that she get home on time. The cold no longer bothered her. She would have liked it if someone were there to share her bottle of rum.

When she finally rose, her legs felt rubbery and the lane on which she walked seem to move back and forth. Despite the liquor that dulled her senses, she knew that a terrible whipping awaited her. Her father would still be up, waiting for her to return. He'd smell the liquor and he would hit her. Katie knew he would hit her several times. As she staggered toward her home even the whipping didn't seem to matter.

CHAPTER FOUR

Katie tried to be more careful about her drinking after the whipping on the night she went to the dance with Rod. Her father's anger had been the worst that she had ever seen. The hitting and slapping had become so severe that even Lucy stepped in to bring it to a stop. Long sleeved blouses would not hide the marks following the whipping, and Katie had to stay home from school for several weeks. Lucy had sent a note saying that Katie had to travel to another city to help one of her aunts who was dying. Missing six weeks of school meant that Katie would fail for the semester. Failing in school was very close to the last straw for Katie. The final incident, though, that sent her running away once again came about because of the broken dishes.

While the bruises healed, Katie spent her days helping Lucy keep the house clean and cooking the evening meal. Since Katie was going to be home from school for such a long time, Lucy decided that everything in the house would be cleaned from top to bottom. Katie's first chore was to empty the kitchen cabinets and to clean all the shelves.

As they cleaned, Lucy and Katie had very little to say to each other. Now and then Lucy would remind Katie about the evils of drinking. "I came from a home where liquor and getting drunk were the two most important things in my parents' lives. I sure don't want a daughter doing the same thing. Can't you see, Katie, you're going to ruin your life? Your father was just trying to get you to see the evil of your ways."

"Drinking makes me feel good." Katie removed all the spices from the lower shelf and wiped the formica clean. "I get down about so many things, and the whiskey makes everything seem okay."

"What do you mean you get down?" Lucy frowned at Katie.

"Sad and all. Kind of depressed."

"A girl your age doesn't have any business getting depressed. You just wait until you see what the problems of the world are really like. Being no older than what you are, you don't have any right to be depressed."

Lucy set her rag down and leaned on the counter. "It just baffles me how I ended up with a child such as you. You're more trouble than all the rest of them put together. Do you see Betsy or Janie acting this way? And your brother Bobbie, why he never does a thing wrong. You're just into one mess after another. I sometimes think the best thing to do with you is just to have you locked up some place until you grow up."

"You're probably right, Mom." Katie squeezed out the extra water in the dishrag. More than anything she wished her mother hadn't been right and that she could be more like her sisters. Her last comment, though, was to defend herself. "You just don't know all the stuff they do. They never get caught and I do."

Lucy poked her finger in Katie's back. "And what does that prove?"

Katie shrugged and moved away from her mother's

glare. "Nothing. I guess."

"It proves that you aren't even as smart as they are. If they can get away with things and not get caught, more power to them. I think what we need to get you for Christmas is some brain cells." Lucy laughed at what she thought was a funny remark. "I wonder how you wrap up brain cells." She laughed again. "Now get all the corners and don't do anything halfway." Lucy draped her wet rag across the sink. "I'll leave you to finish up the shelves and I'll get started in the bathroom."

It was almost eleven by the time Katie started on the shelves that contained the dishes. She noticed that one of the supports holding the shelf in place was broken and the shelf wobbled. "Mom. Mom, there's something wrong with this shelf. It doesn't look right."

Lucy called from the other room. "Those shelves have been there for nearly twenty years. There's nothing wrong with them. Just finish your work and quit complaining."

Katie took the dishes out and and wiped the shelves clean. When the last dish was put back on the shelf, the back corner of the shelf gave way and the dishes came crashing onto the floor. Katie jumped back and covered her mouth with her hands. "Oh, my God!" She quickly knelt down and tried to pick up the pieces of the dozens of dishes that lay cracked and broken on the floor. Katie whispered to herself what she would say to her mother. *Mom, I didn't mean to do it. Honestly, Mom. It just happened.*

Hearing the noise, Lucy instantly ran to the kitchen. "I don't believe it." Lucy eyed the dangling shelf and the pieces of dishes. She shoved Katie aside. "I just don't believe you could have done anything so stupid." She took Katie by the shoulders and shook her. "Do you realize how long your father and me have had those dishes? They were a wedding present." Tears came to Lucy's eyes. "You did this deliberately because you're mad at me and your dad. Well, I'll tell you something, you're not getting away with it."

Katie felt sick to her stomach and her hands trembled. "I didn't do it deliberately," she shouted. "I told you there was something wrong with the shelf support. The shelf was all wobbly. I knew the dishes were going to fall because the shelf was broken."

"That's exactly what I mean. You *knew* they were going to fall and you deliberately put them back."

"But, Mom, you told me to put them back."

Lucy once again shook Katie. "I never said any such thing. I told you to finish your work."

"If I finished my work that meant I was supposed to put the dishes back." Katie felt like her head was going to explode. "The dishes would be back on the shelves if my work was finished. Wouldn't they, Mom? Wouldn't everything be back where it belongs if I finished my work?"

"Get out of here. I can't even stand looking at you." Lucy knelt down and touched the broken dishes. "My three best friends gave me these dishes when I was a bride. All these years I've had these dishes, and now my stupid daughter has broken them. Katie, I'll never forgive you for this. Never."

Katie backed out of the kitchen. Tears ran down her face as she heard her mother's warning about what was going to happen to her when her father got home. Katie ran her fingers down the existing bruises and red marks on her arms and shoulder. The last thing she wanted was another whipping and more bruises, yet she knew that was what awaited her. By the time her mother finished telling her version of the story to Katie's father, Katie was sure it would come out as if Katie had thrown the dishes on the floor.

It was nearly one o'clock when Katie began filling grocery bags with her belongings. This time she knew that she would be gone a long time, and it was best for her to take as much with her as she could take. Katie listened to her mother crying and cursing as she cleaned the bathroom. Quietly Katie moved toward the front door, fearing this time her mother might try to stop her if she heard her leaving. Once out the door, Katie ran as fast she could with the heavy bags. She was out of breath and still shaking when she walked up to the gas station where Gary Churchill worked.

Katie nodded her head at him. Then she went inside the small station and picked up a candy bar to eat while she waited for him to finish waiting on a customer.

"What's up?" Gary munched on a cupcake.

"I left."

"You coming back to our place?"

"No. Tania is still mad at me. Besides, I don't like that jerk she goes with. She doesn't have any time for me ever since she started going with him. Ugh. I just don't see what she sees in that blubber butt."

"I didn't even know Tania had a boyfriend."

"Well, she does. An ugly, stupid creep."

"So where you going?"

"Remember what you said about running away?"

"No." Gary picked up another package of cupcakes. "Why? What did I say?"

"You said you wanted to go to Canada. Do you still want to go?"

"I just got a raise." Chocolate ran down the side of Gary's mouth as he munched down on the last of the cupcake. "I said that quite a while ago."

"Then I guess you didn't mean what you said about running away."

"Listen, I'm eighteen. Guys my age don't run away as you keep calling it. We just up and leave home because we're adults. It's punk kids like you who got to run away. With me it would be an adventure. I always wanted to go to another country. That would be kind of exciting."

"So how come you changed your mind?"

Gary glanced up and saw another car pull into the station. "Let me think about it." He dashed out the door.

Katie opened up a soda and looked at the maps inside the glass case. She slid the case open and took out one that showed the northwestern states, which bordered Canada. Even if Gary didn't want to go, Katie had decided she would go alone.

The map was spread out on the top of the counter when Gary came back inside. "Planning the trip are you?"

"You got a problem with that?" Katie traced her finger along the highways that stretched up through Michigan. "It looks like a long way." Her courage was fading at the thought of traveling so far by herself.

"I got this cousin. Billy. He's not too smart, but he's got a car and he likes to hang out. If I can get him to go with us, we got ourselves some transportation. If he won't go, I'm not going. I don't want to hitchhike that far. It can get pretty dangerous out there. It wasn't that long ago they had that story in the paper about that McDowell kid that got killed hitchhiking."

"The one they found in the woods or by the lake or wherever it was?"

"Yeah. He'd been stabbed. You can't trust these people that pick you up. Some of them are pretty weird." Gary folded up the map. "Let me give Billy a call tonight and see what he says. You'll probably like him. He's a lot of fun. Kind of crazy, but fun."

Katie stayed at the gas station until Gary's shift was over. "I guess I'll come by your place until we find out about Billy. If he doesn't want to go, I got to start making some of my own plans. I just can't go back home."

"What started it this time?"

"I broke a bunch of dishes."

"On purpose?"

Katie thought for a minute. "I guess so," she admitted. "I should have been more careful. They were a wedding present to my mom. They just fell and broke when the shelf collapsed."

"That's not your fault." Gary sympathized with her.

"Yeah. It is. I did something stupid when I put the dishes back on the broken shelf. It's like my mom and dad say. I just don't think most of the time." Katie followed him into the house. As usual, the house was dirty and smelly. "I'd think you'd be glad to get away from this place as nasty as it is."

"It's okay. No one around here cares, anyhow." Gary flopped down into a chair and turned on the television. "I might tell my mom where I'm going. She'd probably worry."

A look of sadness crossed her face. "I wish my parents would worry about me. They don't even care what happens to me." Katie slipped off her shoes and leaned back on the sofa. "I guess if I had a daughter like me, I wouldn't care either."

They watched television for a while. Then Katie went into the kitchen to fix supper. "I might as well cook up something for you guys as long as I'm sitting around doing nothing."

"Hey," Gary glanced at his watch, "Billy ought to be home by now. I'll give him a call."

Katie could not make out his mumbled words as Gary talked to his cousin. All she could do was hope that the young man would go with them. Katie could not bare the thought of staying at Tania's again; going home was out of the question; and leaving for Canada by herself seemed too frightening.

"Okay," Gary called from the other room. "We're on."

Katie set down the potato that she was peeling. "He's going to go?"

"Billy thought the idea was great. What do you say about Wednesday?"

"Perfect."

"Billy's got to get some dough together. Listen, speaking of dough, do you have any or are you going to freeload?"

"I got a few dollars. Maybe twenty." For the first time it struck Katie how poorly she had planned. If she had given any thought at all to her plans, she would have known that she needed money. "What do you think we'll need for the trip?"

Gary twirled his shoe around on his toe. "Oh, I don't know. I'd say two or three hundred."

"For all of us?" The amount he named seemed like a great fortune.

"Naw. Each. Billy's probably got more than that. I can take a couple a hundred out of my savings. Now what about you?"

"I can get it."

"Where?"

"I got three days. I can boost a lot of cigarettes and liquor in three days. There are plenty of kids who'll buy the stuff from me. It's not a problem."

"Don't be going and getting yourself locked up before we even get out of here."

"I said it wasn't a problem."

Katie didn't really mind shoplifting. What she hated was bargaining with the students at school. This time she had to be very careful to stay a safe distance away from the school building. The last thing she needed was to be seen by any of her teachers. When Katie showed up at the sandwich shop where many of the students went to eat lunch, several of the them asked her about the rumor. Most had heard that she wasn't in school because she was pregnant. Katie laughed, denying what they said by showing her flat stomach.

"Never mind about me and babies. You got three bucks for this?" Katie whipped out the liquor that she had hidden under her coat. Despite all her trips to the stores to steal, and her clever bargaining with the students, by Wednesday she only had ninety dollars.

Gary looked at the wad of money that Katie had rolled up in her hand on Wednesday morning. "I thought you told me not to worry about you getting the money. Looks like you're a little short."

"So I'm short. I won't eat much. Besides, I can get a job when we get to Canada."

Gary shook his head. "You got a lot to learn, chick. You can't work in Canada."

"And why not?"

"You can't work in a foreign country. It's against the law."

"Whose law?"

"How do I know whose law." Gary looked annoyed. "I just know it for a fact. Something about immigration or passports. Stuff like that."

"Then I'll get a job in Michigan before we get to Canada."

"Hey, Billy and me aren't going to be sitting around while you're trying to get your act together. We're heading for Canada for some adventure."

Katie had some questions as it began to strike her about the future. "How long we going to be there?"

Gary shrugged. "How do I know. As long as the adventure and the money lasts. Why do you want to know?"

"I don't ever want to come back."

"Well, I'm coming back. I'm not leaving forever as you say. I got no problem with my family. You're the one with the problems."

"I'm staying once we get there."

"Suit yourself." Gary went to his bedroom to pack what he was going to take with him. Then he heard the pounding on the front door. "Get that. It's probably Billy."

Katie opened the door and saw a tall, freckled, and very red-headed young man. "Are you Billy?"

"Yeah. Who wants to know?" He stalked into the living room. "Where's Gary?"

Katie eyed him from head to foot. She didn't like red hair, but she had to admit that he was very nice looking. "Gary's getting his stuff."

"Back here, Billy. Be right with you and we'll head out. That's Katie. She's going with us."

Billy frowned. "You didn't say anything about no girl going with us."

"She's got to get away from her family. You know how that goes. Her mom and dad are nuts."

Katie started to shout to him that her family wasn't nuts. Then Gary appeared in the living room. She asked, "How come you didn't tell him about me?"

"I figured he might not go if he knew you were coming. Listen, Billy, she won't be any trouble. She can steal stuff faster than you can blow your nose. Just about anything we need, Katie can get it for us."

Billy asked, "Is that true?"

"I'm pretty good at it." Katie tried to smile, but she didn't like Billy's scowling face.

"Okay, so let's get out of here."

Katie picked up her bags, pleased that Billy had not put up more of a protest. "I won't be any trouble."

"You better not be. Me and Gary got this adventure

planned. If you don't fit in, you're out."

"Out where?" Katie had visions of his throwing her out of the car on some lonely road along the way.

Gary slapped her shoulder. "Quit worrying. Billy's not going to dump you. He's kidding."

Katie followed them down the gravel sidewalk to the car. She pitched her bags in the backseat and crawled into the car. "Go past my house. I want to see if anyone is in the yard or anything."

Gary turned around and stared at her. "What do you want to do that for?"

"Because I'm probably not going to see them ever again."

"You ought to be glad."

Katie sat forward and peered out the back window. She thought Gary should be right. She ought to be glad that she wasn't going to see them again, and yet the thought made her sad. More than anything she wished she could be the type of daughter they wanted so that she wouldn't have to run away all the time. The trip to Canada, though, Katie was sure would be different. This time they would not know where she was and she did not plan to come back. There was some sense of happiness in Katie's mind as they drove past the small bungalow where she lived. Perhaps this time her parents would miss her and regret that they had not at least said goodbye.

CHAPTER FIVE

Most of the trip north was boring to Katie. By the second day on the road, her voice was hoarse from trying to talk above the loud music that Billy played constantly on the radio or on the tape player. She wrapped herself in a blanket and slept most of the time. When she stirred awake, she listened to the two young men talk about girls or about what they were going to do in Canada as part of their adventure. Their plans sounded much like the plans they might make at home: They wanted to drink and find girls. Katie wondered what she would do while Billy and Gary went in pursuit of the females that would occupy so much of their time.

Katie leaned forward to put her chin on the back of their seat. "You guys are all the same. Don't you ever think about anything but drinking and chasing skirts?" She stretched her arms up as high as she could reach. "I'm getting tired of being cooped up in the car."

Billy turned around and patted her on the head. "If you'd give me a tumble, I wouldn't have to be hunting down these chicks."

"Ho. Hum. Don't be boring me with your come-on." Katie smiled. She liked teasing Billy. She also knew that once he had become used to her presence, he had started flirting with her. It crossed her mind that he was cute, and his liking her was almost like a guarantee that he wouldn't dump her some place as he had threatened to do the first time she met him.

Billy reached across the front seat and opened the glove compartment. "Here. I'll show you something that won't bore you." He took out a black gun. "Look at that handle, will you. My uncle says it's pearl."

"No thanks." Katie pushed it away. "I hate guns."

Gary stroked the gun. "Hey, Billy, where did you get this? It's something else."

Billy seemed pleased that Gary admired the gun. "My uncle's. He's got this whole gun collection. He'll never miss it."

Katie pulled away from the front seat. "What do we need a gun for?"

Billy turned around and grinned at her. "Who knows why we might need a gun. We could shoot a bear or we might shoot someone who's trying to steal our car. Some hoods could be trying to do us in. I just feel safer with a gun." Billy slowed down and pulled over to the side of the road. "Put it in your purse." He nudged Katie's knee with the gun.

"No way. I'm not putting any gun in my purse." Katie drew away from him.

"What's your problem?" Gary asked.

Katie's voice showed her annoyance. "I don't have any problem, as you say. I just don't want to be toting any gun around. Besides, Billy, why do you want me to put the stupid thing in my purse?"

"It will be safer with you. No one is going to search any girl's purse looking for a gun."

"Who is going to be searching my purse, anyhow?" Katie looked puzzled.

"You never know. Listen," Billy was becoming equally annoyed. "We're going to some foreign country. You don't know how they feel about Americans. They might try to shoot us or something."

Katie crossed her arms over her chest. "You're crazy, Billy. I've seen all kinds of pictures of Canada. Their cities are just like our cities. I bet you wouldn't be able to tell one bit of difference between someone who lives in Canada and us."

Billy reached over and shook Katie's shoulder. "I'll tell you one difference. We're going to have a gun to protect ourselves. Now put this in your purse or I'm throwing you out of the car. I mean it, Katie. I'll dump your butt right out on the road."

Listening to him was like listening to her father. Always the threats. She wondered if anyone would ever talk nicely to her. "So give me the gun."

"That's more like it." Billy opened his hand and the gun lay in full view.

"Does it have bullets in it?" Katie gingerly picked up the gun by the barrel.

"Don't hold it like that!" Billy shouted at her. "And, no, it doesn't have bullets in it. You think I'm crazy or something. You don't carry around a loaded gun. Someone could get hurt."

"I thought you could put bullets in it and then you did

66

something to make sure it didn't go off or anything." Katie dropped the gun into her purse. "I see them doing that on TV all the time. They click something and then they can shoot."

"It's called a safety." Gary smiled at her. "You got a lot to learn."

"The less I learn about guns, the happier I'll be." Katie pushed her purse to the other side of the seat. "I'm getting hungry and tired."

"You sleep all the time." Billy turned on the engine and pulled back onto the highway. "We'll get in another hour on the road. Then we can stop for some chow. Maybe drive another four hours or so. What do you say Scary-Gary?"

"Sounds okay to me." Gary dropped his head down against the seat. "Let's stop some place tonight. I don't want to sleep in the car again."

Like Katie, Gary dozed until he felt the motion of the car stop. Billy pulled into a fast-food restaurant and placed an order for the three of them.

Katie rummaged through the bag that Billy handed her. "You didn't even ask me what I wanted. I hate mustard on my hamburger."

"Quit complaining and eat it."

As Katie chomped down on the hamburger, she thought how being with Billy and Gary wasn't much different than being with her parents. There were never choices for her to make, and there always was something that she was doing wrong or some remark about something that she said. Katie sighed and took another bite. She concluded there must be more things wrong with her than she thought. If her parents, and now her friends, believed she was stupid and complaining, then that's how she must be.

"I guess the mustard wasn't too bad." Katie smiled a weak smile of apology. "I'm sorry I was such a stinkpot about the gun. I mean what's it to me if the gun's in my purse."

"Hey, listen," Billy liked it that she had regrets. "You're okay, Katie. I mean you need to listen a little more, but basically, you're okay."

The sun had set and it had long since grown dark before Billy pulled into a motel. "This place looks cheap. You two get down. I'll pay for one. Then the both of you can sneak in." Billy walked to the office to check in. In a few minutes he returned with a key. "That guy is a no-good. He said he didn't like letting rooms to punks. They tear up the place."

"Then how come he let you have a room?" Gary lay hunched on the floor.

"You see any other cars around here? The old coot probably hasn't had anyone else stop. Who'd stay at a dump like this?" He pulled the car in front of a small, dingy, and poorly lit cabin. "I can smell the place from here." Billy opened the car door. "Wait about ten minutes and then run for the door."

Katie remained in a huddled position until she was sure ten minutes had passed. "Let's go." She pushed open the door and dashed for the cabin. Once inside, she was overcome with the smell. "This is nasty!" She pinched her nose closed.

Gary gave her a shove. "There you go again. Always complaining."

"Well, Mr. Gary, considering how you live at home, you wouldn't notice that this place is filthy and that it stinks." Katie moved toward the tiny bathroom. "Oh, Lord! There's bugs crawling all over the place. Roaches and those silverfish things." She sucked in her breath and closed the door while she used the toilet. When she came out and looked around at the room, she knew she would have to sleep on the floor as there was only one bed. "Can I have one of the blankets?"

Billy pulled down the spread. "We only got one blanket."

"Then give me the spread." Katie grabbed the stained spread from the bed. "I'm not sleeping on that putrid rug. It looks like it hasn't been cleaned or vacuumed since before I was born." Katie knelt down and folded the spread in half. "I don't suppose I can have a pillow?"

"You got that right." Billy stuffed his fist back and forth in the flat pillow, trying to fluff it up. "I drove all day, and I put out the money for this place. I need my beauty rest."

For most of the night Katie tossed back and forth on

the hard floor. When she rolled to her stomach, her nose pressed against the horrid-smelling carpet. When she moved to her back, she ached from the hardness of the floor.

"What's the matter? You can't sleep." Billy whispered and knelt down beside her.

Katie immediately sensed she was in some kind of danger. "You get away from me, Billy." The spread seemed to offer her very little protection. "I'm sleeping just fine."

"You know I really like you, Katie." He moved closer to her, dropping his voice to an even lower whisper.

"If you don't get away from me, I'm going to scream and get Gary up and get that old coot in here."

Billy placed his hand across Katie's mouth. "You better listen to me, stupid. No one says I got to take you along. I'm doing it as a favor to Gary. I don't owe you nothing."

"I didn't say you did." Katie scooted away from him. The look on his face frightened her.

"Even though you're not the brightest person in the world, you ought to have this figured out."

"I do. Get away from me."

"You ought to be glad a guy like me is interested in you because what other guy is ever going to want you." Billy felt pleased that he knew exactly what to say to make her feel terrible about herself.

Katie bit on the edge of the blanket. She could feel

one of her panic attacks coming on. Those were something that had been bothering her for several months. A feeling of fear would simply grab at her. There was some terrible kind of feeling that she would never please anyone, and that she would never be loved. Her blood would race and perspiration quickly seemed to come out of every pore in her body. "Please leave me alone, Billy. I just want to get to sleep."

"Well, how would you like to get left here? Come on, Katie, how would you like that?" His hand went to her shoulder and then to stroking her hair.

"You wouldn't do that to me."

He again placed his hand across her mouth. "Keep your voice down. Honest to God, I never met a girl as stupid as you."

When he said the word *stupid*, Katie winced. Was there anyone in the world who didn't think she was stupid? "I'm sorry." Katie could not understand why she apologized to the very young man who was now threatening her. "If I'm so stupid, then why do you want to do this to me?"

"Just shut up, or you'll find yourself having to find a way to work your way out of this town."

In the morning Katie could not look at either Billy or Gary. All she could feel was disgust at herself. She went into the bathroom and washed herself over and over again, hoping that she could wash away the memory of Billy's touching her.

Gary shouted and pounded on the door. "You think

71

you own that john? Come on, Katie, we all got to use the toilet."

Katie leaned over the sink and threw up. Again and again she gagged. She was sure if she stood up that she would faint. Her hands grasped the edge of the sink as she fought to keep herself from having another panic attack. "I'll be right out." Katie barely whispered the words.

Gary looked at her when she emerged from the bathroom. "You sure didn't spend anytime fixing yourself up. You look downright awful." He pushed past her. "What you'd do in here Katie? It smells like puke."

Katie leaned over to pick up and fold the spread. Billy tried to stroke her shoulder. "Don't touch me!" She pushed his hand away. "Don't ever touch me again!" Her lips twisted in anger.

"You should see yourself, Katie. You look plain old ugly. No one would want to touch you."

The blood raced to Katie's head and her hands were wet with perspiration. She could only breathe by taking deep gulps of air.

"What's wrong with you, Katie?" Gary showed some sympathy as he looked at her pale face and saw her trying to suck in air. "You get sick sleeping on that floor or something?"

"I want to go home." That was all Katie kept uttering for the next few minutes while they waited for Billy to come out of the bathroom.

"Shut up about that." Gary stood over her. "You were

the one who wanted to come on this trip We're sure not turning around now. We're heading for Canada."

"Please, Gary. I got to get home."

"Well, you can forget about that because we're not going back. Billy will kill you if you keep running your mouth about going home."

Katie started sobbing. "Then I'm going by myself." She grabbed her purse and ran out the door.

After a few minutes of walking along the highway, she heard the honking of a horn. Katie turned around and saw Billy's car approaching. Fearing that she had made the wrong choice, and wondering how she would ever make it home by herself, Katie tried to flag down Billy and Gary. Billy stopped for a second, rolled down the window, and shouted, "Hey, stupid, you're heading in the wrong direction." He gave the horn a honk and sped off.

For several minutes Katie stood along the side of the road thinking they would come back for her. The cold, northerly wind pierced right through her thin jacket. When she turned around, she no longer could see the horrid cabins where they had stayed. Then she realized that she had walked a long way, and that Gary and Billy were not coming back for her. Only two cars passed her during the entire morning. Both drivers turned to look back at the girl making her way along the highway. Neither driver bothered to stop.

Katie estimated that it must be getting close to noon because she was so hungry. All she could remember was that last night they had driven through a small town just before they had reached the cabin. The distance they traveled in the car didn't seem very far. Walking in the cold, blustery wind made the distance seem so terribly much longer. She reached in her bag and pulled out a sweater. Katie yanked the sweater right over her jacket, wrapping one more sweater around her head.

The sun had moved farther into the western sky by the time she saw the edge of town. She breathed a sigh of relief knowing that in just a few minutes she would be inside a restaurant where she could get warm and get something to eat.

Her appearance in the doorway of the restaurant caused a few customers to turn and look at her. She was not properly dressed for such a cold climate, and the sweater sleeves tied beneath her chin brought smiles to the faces of the other diners. Katie slid into a booth in the back of the restaurant and sucked in the smell of food.

The waitress placed a napkin and silverware in front of Katie. "Do you need a menu?"

"Do you have any hot soup?"

"You know of any other kind." The waitress grinned.

Embarrassed at her thoughtless question, Katie lowered her eyes so that she didn't have to look at the waitress. "What kind do you have?"

"Vegetable. Chicken. Cream of potato."

"I'll have vegetable. And crackers, too."

"All the soup comes with crackers. Anything else?"

Wondering how long her money was going to last worried Katie. She thought it best to order only what was absolutely necessary to get her to the next meal. "That's all."

The waitress stood over Katie for a few more seconds. "You're a runaway, aren't you?"

A feeling of tenseness swept over Katie. All she could think to do was order more food. "Maybe I'll have a piece of pie. Do you have apple pie?"

"Yeah. We got apple pie." The waitress walked away.

The soup tasted delicious, warming Katie as it made its way to her stomach. As she lifted her fork to begin eating the pie, she saw the man in a tan uniform. Then Katie noticed the waitress nod in the direction of the booth where Katie sat. Long before he walked over to sit down, Katie knew that he had come to the restaurant because of her.

He slid into the other side of the booth and smiled. "They got mighty good pie in this place."

Katie nodded, fearing that if she looked up, he would know her whole life story.

"You live around here?"

"No." Katie offered no other information.

"Traveling through?"

"Yes."

"Got a name and an address?"

Katie barely whispered her name and mumbled her address.

"You a runaway?"

"No."

"Can you do a little more explaining to me?" His voice was not stern or frightening, yet Katie trembled every time he spoke.

"My friends are driving me to my aunt's. She's really sick. My mom sent me to take care of her."

"And where are your friends?"

At this moment, Katie wished she knew. "They drove up the road. I had this little fight with my boyfriend. He's sort of bent out of shape about it, but he'll be back for me."

"And how old is the boyfriend?" The deputy picked up the cup of coffee the waitress had set in front of him.

Katie thought it best to say twenty-five so that the deputy wouldn't think she was traveling with another minor.

"That's a little old for you. How old are you?"

"Twenty," Katie lied.

"They must make them younger looking south of here." He stirred the coffee before taking a sip. "You know I deal with a lot of kids, and from what I know about kids, I sure am sitting here thinking that you're lying to me."

"Oh, no." Katie finally looked at him. "I'm going to take care of my aunt. In fact, I better get outside because my boyfriend is probably going to be back for me any second now." Katie scooted across the seat, knocking her purse to the floor. The gun clunked out and slid across the floor.

In seconds the deputy was out of the booth and had picked up the gun. "Well, I expect this here gun is going to make your story a little more interesting."

Katie had forgotten all about the gun. "That's not mine. It belongs to Billy."

"The boyfriend?"

Katie shivered at the thought of Billy and what he had done to her. "No." Her voice trembled. "I hate Billy." Her eyes filled with tears thinking about how she hoped she would never see him again.

"I'd like to get it across to you, young lady, that I'm here to help you. We see a lot of what goes on when you kids get yourself in jams. We don't want any runaway kids having problems in this town. It can get mighty dangerous out there by yourself." He put the gun in his coat pocket. "Now why don't you sit down and finish that pie of yours. Then we'll be going over to my office and doing a little more talking."

Katie dropped back onto the edge of the booth. "What kind of talking?" She felt quite bold in asking the question.

"Like how you come by this gun, and how I can help you to get back to where it is you belong."

She picked up the fork and tried to eat the pie. The pains in her stomach wouldn't go away. "That might be a problem, Sir."

"Why's that?"

Tears ran down her cheek. "I don't think you're going

to figure out where I belong. I been trying to figure that one out for most of my life."

CHAPTER SIX

As the plane took off, Katie wrapped her fingers around the arm rest of her seat. The sound of the plane getting ready to take off had frightened her. Its speed down the runway and its sudden rise above the clouds only added to her fear.

For two days she had felt nothing but fear. First there was the endless questioning by the sheriff's deputy, who repeated again and again that he only wanted to help her. Fear and weariness finally wore her down, and by late afternoon on the day the deputy had brought her in, Katie told her full story. She said nothing of what Billy had done to her. Katie related only how she wanted to run away to Canada.

There was the phone call to her parents. When the deputy put down the receiver, he had a better understanding of why the young girl had run away. The cold, disinterested attitude of the girl's mother bothered him. Her first question had nothing to do with whether Katie was hurt or safe. Mrs. Bennett asked only if it were going to cost her any money to bring Katie back.

Katie sat across from the deputy as he placed the call. In her heart she knew her mother had not asked much about her. Yet, when the deputy hung up, Katie leaned forward and inquired, "Did she want to know if I was okay?"

The deputy lied. "She's real worried about you." He dropped his head so that the girl couldn't tell he was lying. The deputy could not help but think how he would feel if one of his own children were several hundred miles from home sitting in the office of a law enforcement agent. He'd probably be crying, he thought, and Katie's mother mentioned only that her daughter had no business doing what she had done, and that there would be a price to pay when she got home.

He wanted to put his arm around the girl and tell her that everything was going to be all right, but he knew that would be a bigger lie than the one he had just told her. "I think what we're going to do is contact the juvenile authorities back where you live. Maybe it's time we brought some others into this situation of yours."

Katie wondered what situation he meant. "You mean like the police?"

He didn't want to frighten her more than she was already frightened. "Not exactly. This running away is getting pretty serious what with you out on the highways by yourself. There's no telling what could have happened to you. A young girl like yourself belongs in school. We got to put an end to this running away. That's not going to solve anything."

Katie let out a deep sigh. "I can't go back to school. I'm going to really get a whipping for all this trouble I caused my mom and dad. They're not going to let me go back to school for a long time." She didn't say a word about the fact she would be out of school until the bruises left by her father had disappeared. "I just know I'm going to be in real deep trouble when I get home."

"That's why we want a juvenile officer involved. Besides," he glanced at Katie, "carrying a concealed weapon is a crime. That issue has to be settled. Someone back there might want to press some charges."

"What does that mean?"

"It means you might be going to some place where you'll be incarcerated."

"What's that?" Katie felt uneasy about the word even if she didn't know what it meant.

The deputy hesitated to give her the meaning. "Locked up."

"Me! You mean I might go to jail!" Katie twisted her fingers together and wished that she could get to her bottle of rum or whiskey.

"No. Oh, no." He lowered his voice and tried to sound comforting. "Some type of juvenile home. Maybe a foster home. I don't know how your juvenile system works." He was sure that no matter how the system worked, it would be better for the girl to be in the hands of the juvenile authorities than it would be to deal with her parents. Without getting too involved, the deputy said, "You know you don't have to put up with those whippings." It angered him that any parent would seek a solution by beating a child. "That's one of the things we need to get investigated. The abuse."

Katie thought about the word *abuse*. She never thought of herself as abused. "My mom and dad are just trying to help me. You see, sir, I'm always in trouble. I'm not too smart. I cause them a lot of problems."

Her defense of her mother and father only made him feel worse. She had been brainwashed into believing that what they did to her was her fault. "Well, before you do anymore defending of what they do, maybe we ought to be looking into the situation just a bit more."

The deputy helped her on with her coat. Then he took her to his house and turned her over to his wife for the night. "I still got a few calls to make. It's my plan to put you on a plane in the morning."

When Katie stood in line waiting for the passengers to board the plane, she felt as if she were going to throw up. The deputy patted her on the shoulder and told her there was nothing to be afraid of. Then he handed her a card with his name and address on it. "Here, Katie, put this in that purse of yours. You give me a call if anyone back there doesn't do right by you. I want to keep in touch and find out what happens. Okay?"

Katie looked at the card. *Eldon Crowley.* "You're Eldon?"

"That's right. I got kids of my own. They're grown now, but I had to get through some problems with them. I'm a man who likes kids."

"You've been nice to me." Katie knew the line was moving and soon she would have to board the plane. "I never flew before. I'm scared."

"You're going to be fine. Now you take care, kid, and keep in touch." He watched her go through the entrance to board the plane. He knew she was a decent girl who needed a break in life. More than anything, he hoped the authorities waiting at the other end would give her that break.

All through the flight Katie sat stiff and rigid in her seat, wishing nothing more than that the plane would land. When the wheels of the plane finally touched down, she let out a gasp. Picking up her two paper bags, she jumped out of her seat as soon as the other passengers stood up.

As soon as Katie entered the terminal, an attractive blond woman approached her. "Are you Katie Bennett?"

Katie shifted her bags. "Yes." She looked at the woman. Her pretty face made it impossible for Katie to believe that the woman could do her any harm.

"I'm Lucia Cavanaugh. I'm with the juvenile court. Deputy Crowley contacted us. This way, sweetie." Lucia pointed toward the exit. "Did you have any luggage?"

"This." Katie nodded her head downward to indicate she meant her paper bags. Then Katie looked around. "Is my mom here?"

Lucia could see the look of disappointment on the girl's face. Deputy Crowley had warned Lucia that the girl came from a home where there was a good chance that physical abuse was taking place. Instantly Lucia felt a sense of sadness for the girl. Katie was like so many of the other youngsters with whom she dealt . They had been mistreated, and still they sought and craved the love of the very people who were harming them.

"You'll see your parents after we get you to our office. They've been notified that you'll be there." Lucia thought it best that the first contact Katie had with her parents should be in the presence of a juvenile officer.

"Are they pretty mad?"

Lucia spoke truthfully. "I think you could say that they are upset."

"Upset or mad?"

"Maybe a little of both."

"I really did it this time, didn't I?" Katie once again shifted her bags. "Do they know about the gun?"

"They know why you were picked up, and that includes having the gun."

Katie sighed deeply. "My dad is going to kill me."

If Lucia had her way, it would be quite a while before her father was alone with Katie. It was Lucia's intention to have Katie turned over to the court for the purpose of counseling her, seeing that she attended school, and that she be protected from her parents. The only way to do that, Lucia knew, was to have Katie placed at the detention center.

The first meeting Katie had with her mother and father went as Lucia expected it would go. The Bennetts entered the room where Katie sat huddled in her chair. There were no warm greetings, no hugs, and no crying. The first words out of her father's mouth were words of warning and about the shame that Katie had caused them. Mrs. Bennett added nothing to the welcome. She shook her head again and again, complaining repeatedly that of all her children, Katie caused her the most problems. Katie also did as Lucia expected. She said she was sorry. She apologized for being so much trouble. She made promises about how she'd clean the house and cook every meal to make up for what she had done. What Katie said fell on deaf ears. Neither her father nor mother accepted her apologies. No sooner had Katie finished speaking, when one or the other of her parents had a story to tell about how she had upset them.

Lucia brought the meeting to an end as quickly as she could. She warned the Bennetts that there was a good chance that Katie would be sent to Lake Woods, the juvenile detention center. "I think it will help her rather than hurt her."

Mrs. Bennett reached over and shook Katie's shoulder. "*Now* see what you've done. You've turned yourself into a criminal. Now doesn't that beat all. One of our children is going to prison. How are we going to explain that to everyone? Just answer me that, Katie."

Lucia didn't allow for an answer. The parents had done nothing but make matters worse. "Katie is not a criminal, Mrs. Bennett, and she's not going to a prison. Let's not make things worse than they already are."

Mr. Bennett wanted the last word. "And how can things get any worse?"

Lucia wanted to say things could get worse if Katie were released to them, but she silenced herself. "There just comes a time when it's necessary for the authorities to step in. Sometimes the parents and the kids just can't work things out. Matters have gotten out of hand. By our working with Katie, we hope to get matters back on track. Sort of teach her how to handle her problems."

"Her problems!" Mr. Bennett sneered at Lucia. "She's not the one with problems. What with a daughter like that, we're the ones with the problems."

"That's very true." Lucia bent her head and smiled. He was exactly right. *They* were the ones with the problems. "You'll be expected to be at the hearing. Katie will be represented by a juvenile officer. That officer will recommend to the courts that she be placed at Lake Woods. You can contest that decision, but I really think it's best at this time to get Katie some help."

Mrs. Bennett glared at Katie. "Well, you can just get us some help while you're at it. Like my husband says, we need more help than any parents alive. In fact, I don't know of too many parents that would put up with a girl like Katie."

Lucia felt nothing but relief when they left. It didn't surprise her, though, that Katie felt sadness when they were gone. Lucia was always baffled by the fact that some parents could insult and hurt their children so much, and the children still fought for the approval of their mothers and fathers.

"Well, so much for that." Lucia gathered together the papers on Katie's case. "Do you feel pretty beat?" From the worn out look on Katie's face, Lucia didn't really need to ask the question.

"Yeah. I guess I'm kind of tired." Katie stood up and stretched. "I shouldn't have done what I did. Taking that gun from Billy was crazy. I just never do anything that's smart. Now my poor mom and dad are going to have to explain to everyone that I'm in prison."

Lucia clenched her hands together. It enraged her that Katie's concern was not for herself, but for her parents. It also angered her that Katie used the word *prison* because that's what her parents had said. "It's not a prison where you're going, Katie. It's not like that at all."

Katie didn't seem to hear her. "My brother and my sisters never seem to get in trouble."

Blaming herself again. "No one is perfect, Katie, and that includes your brother and sisters." Lucia didn't feel it was her place to add that very often a parent would pick out what Lucia thought of as the *victim*. The victim would be the child, who for some unknown reason, a parent had decided to torment. That fact was one that Lucia knew would become apparent in counseling. Katie, Lucia believed, had already been through enough. There was no reason for Lucia to say anything else right now. Besides, Lucia knew that no matter what was said, Katie would end up defending her parents because she still believed they were right and she was wrong.

"You'll be with us a short time, Katie. I'm sorry to say, but the youngsters who are waiting for their court hearings are kept in cells. It's not a very pleasant experience. I'm sorry that it has to be done. After the hearing you'll be taken to Lake Woods. I think you'll like it there. Come along now, we need to get you settled."

Katie picked up her bags and followed Lucia down the hall. No matter how nice Lake Woods would be, Katie wished only that she could go home and be with her family.

CHAPTER SEVEN

As winter turned to spring, Katie's only contact with her parents had consisted of their one visit at Easter and the letters that she wrote to them. There were no answers to her letters except for the notes that Bobbie now and then wrote her. During the first two months that Katie spent at Lake Woods she found out one thing for sure, and one thing that she suspected. The thing that she knew for sure was that she had been wrong about black people, or *Africans,* as her father called all black people. The thing that Katie suspected was that she was pregnant.

Katie remembered back to the first week that she was at Lake Woods. She had no trouble making friends. The others who were her age, and who were there for everything from hitting a principal to running away from home, were quick to make themselves known to Katie. The dorm where Katie slept and lived when not in school or counseling was filled with the noise of other teenage girls.

When Katie first arrived at Lake Woods the thing that bothered her most was finding out that Mary, her teacher, was an *African.* Katie made an attempt to protest to Mr. Calkins that she did not want Mary as her teacher. Mr. Calkins made it clear that the young people at Lake Woods didn't have many choices, and who they would have for a teacher certainly was not among their choices.

Katie entered the classroom and quickly took a seat as far away from Mary as she could get. In spite of Katie's efforts not to like Mary, Katie found that the good-natured

89

teacher had far too many winning ways to ignore. To begin with, Katie found it difficult to accept Mary's compliments on how well Katie was doing in school. Katie didn't know how to deal with compliments. More often than not, Katie would respond to Mary's compliments by saying something negative about herself.

Mary was quick to notice how much difficulty Katie had in accepting any comments that were made to help Katie with her self-esteem. "You know, Darling," Mary's hand stroked Katie's hair, "when someone says something nice about you, you don't have to bark back. All you need to do is say, 'Why thank you. That was nice of you to say that.' Get what I mean?"

Katie pulled her head back. Feeling Mary's hand touching her hair made Katie uncomfortable. "I didn't do all that great."

"That's exactly what I mean." Mary took Katie's chin in her hand. "Do you think I'm just running my mouth when I tell you what a fine job you did?"

"I don't know why you say those things to me." Katie stared at another student who turned around to listen to the conversation between the teacher and the student.

"I say them, child, because they are true. You always hand in good work. There's no reason why you shouldn't be proud of what you do."

"I'm sort of stupid in school."

"Well, you sure could have fooled me." Mary smiled at the young girl who seemed determined to find something bad to say about herself. "What is it there you're working on now?"

"My English paper."

"What are you writing about?"

"It's about black people." Katie realized how much her attitude toward and her beliefs about blacks had changed since she had been at Lake Woods. "Mary, did you know I used to not like you?" After she spoke the words, Katie could almost feel a hand striking against her. Whenever she had spoken the truth in the past, it usually meant she would be hit.

Mary broke out laughing. "Is that a fact?" She picked up Katie's hand and rubbed it against her cheek. "Oh, yes, child, I knew you didn't want to be in here with me. What was it you called me? The *African* teacher."

Katie blushed. "That's what my dad calls black people. He said you all ought to be sent back to Africa where you belong."

"I don't think I'd do any better in Africa than you or your daddy would do. I'm an American just like you, Katie."

"I know that now. You're a nice teacher."

Mary squeezed Katie's hand and let it drop. "Why thank you, Katie. That was nice of you to say that."

Katie grinned. "Is that how you want me to talk?"

"It's not so important, child, how I want you to talk. It's more important how *you* want to talk. It's real important that you believe good things about yourself. You're a very capable girl. Put those capabilities to work for yourself."

"Do you think I'm stupid and clumsy, Mary?"

"And why would I think such things?"

"Because I am."

"I've seen you out on that basketball court. Why you run with the grace of a deer. No, little girl, I don't think you're clumsy. You're very well coordinated."

"How come you came to my basketball game?" Katie found it strange that this teacher whom she had known for only a short time came to the game when her own parents had never seen her play in any game.

"Because you're in my classroom and I wanted to show you that you're just as important to me outside the classroom as you are in it."

"That was nice of you to come." The look on Mary's face made Katie smile.

"Thank you." Mary grinned. "That was nice of you to say that."

The most special time that Katie had with Mary came when Mary asked her if she'd like to go home with her for the weekend. After two months at Lake Woods, Katie was among those youngsters whose parents did not come for them when the youngsters were given leave. Mary knew that Katie's parents had no intention of visiting her on a regular basis, nor did they intend to come and get her so that she could enjoy her weekend pass away from Lake Woods.

"What would we do at your place?" Katie put the question to Mary when she extended her the invitation.

"Oh, I don't think it matters. You can meet my husband and my son. I've told them all about you."

"Maybe they won't like me."

"But why wouldn't they?" Mary watched Katie fold up a few of her things and put them in yet one more paper bag.

Katie shrugged. "I don't know. Mrs. Churchill liked me because I cleaned up their pig pen. Most people, though, don't much take to me."

"I don't know why. You're a lovely young lady."

The color rushed to Katie's face. She smiled and said, "Thank you. That was nice of you to say that."

"Now you got it, child. Take those compliments and run with them."

When Katie walked into Mary's house she was startled. She looked around and everything she saw was beautiful. Her father had told her that blacks lived like pigs. What Katie saw was cleanliness and charm. "It sure is pretty."

The words were barely out of her mouth when Mary's son walked into the living room. He smiled and put his arms around Mary. "Hi, Mom."

Mary kissed him on the cheek. "Martin, I want you to meet Katie. Katie, this is my oldest son." She placed her arm around his waist. "He's a winner, this one is."

Martin extended his hand. "I'm glad to meet you, Katie." His smile was identical to that of Mary's. "Do you smell that stew?" He sniffed. "Dad's been in that kitchen

93

banging those pans around for about an hour. He thought Katie might like some good homemade stew. Do you like stew, Katie?"

Katie nodded. "I love stew." It startled her that the man of the house would be in the kitchen cooking.

"Come along, Katie. I want you to meet one of the greatest cooks in the world." Mary took Katie's hand and pulled her toward the kitchen. "Donald," she called out to her husband. "I want you to meet one of my favorite students."

Mary's husband stood by the stove. He sipped at the stew. "This is going to be a good one." He leaned down and opened the oven door. "I even made homemade bread in honor of our guest." Donald wiped his hands on the towel and reached out to take Katie's hand. "It's a pleasure having you, young lady. I've heard nothing but good things about you."

Katie knew she should thank him, but the words wouldn't come out. "I can set the table."

"No. No." Donald smiled at her. "You're our guest. Now you go along with Mary and sit yourself down. I'll give you a call when it's time to eat."

His warning that dinner would be on the table in five minutes seemed to come shortly after Mary and Katie had sat down to watch the evening news. Katie stood by the table waiting to be told where to sit. Her eyes glowed as she looked at the white linen tablecloth and the candles. "It sure looks pretty."

Donald walked around to seat his wife. Then he nodded to Martin. "Are you forgetting your manners, Son?"

Martin nodded back. "Oh, no, Sir." He motioned for Katie to sit down so that he could push her chair in for her. "Sorry about that."

Katie turned around and looked up at him. She couldn't believe that he was so polite. Katie could see that Mary's family was trying to make her feel comfortable. Every few minutes they asked her a question about herself, and Katie replied with one or two words. She didn't mean to be unfriendly. Katie simply was caught up in listening to this family. They talked so nicely at the dinner table. They talked about school and work and about the news and about their plans. Each of them seemed to take an interest in what the other one said. No one argued about where they would sit. No one yelled because some plate wasn't passed fast enough. Not one unkind thing was said throughout the meal. Katie found the meal so pleasant that she almost could not eat.

"If you don't like the stew, Katie," Donald said, "maybe I can fix you something else."

"Oh, no. It's delicious. I was just listening. I forgot about my supper." She pushed her fork into a potato. "It really is the best stew I ever had."

Mary looked at Katie and smiled. "One of these times when Katie comes to visit we're going to let her cook. She tells me she makes very good chili."

"It's not all that good. It's not like my mom makes or

anything. It's just sort of good."

"Sort of good is good enough for me." Donald reached over and patted Katie's hand.

When the meal was over, Donald and Martin cleaned up the dishes. Katie sat in the living room with Mary and listened to the father and son talking in the kitchen. Their voices were low and pleasant.

Mary sat down on the couch and put her arm around Katie. "Are you enjoying yourself, young lady?"

Katie tilted her head. She still felt uncomfortable when Mary touched her. "Your family seems sort of crazy." As soon as she said the words, Katie knew they should not have been spoken. "Oh, I don't mean nuts or anything like that. Just sort of strange." Her additional explanation sounded as bad as her first statement.

Mary seemed not the least upset. "What is it about us that seems crazy?" She truly wanted to know what Katie thought.

Now Katie felt trapped. She didn't really want to talk about Mary's family. They all had been so nice. The last thing that Katie wanted to do was make Mary angry. "You'll get all mad at me if I say anything."

"I doubt that. You're just expressing your opinion. You do have a right to an opinion. That surely isn't going to make me angry."

Katie took a deep breath. She was sure that Mary probably never became angry about anything. "You're always kissing and hugging each other. That's not normal.

96

And no one ever yells at anyone. You talk funny. Like you're not mad at each other or something like that."

"But we're not mad at each other." Mary could feel only sympathy for the girl. "I kiss and hug my son and husband because I love them. Those are two ways that I can show them that I care about them."

"My mom and dad never kiss and hug me."

"Does it bother you that they don't?"

"Heck. I don't know."

Mary glanced at the arm that she rested on Katie's shoulder. "Do you mind it when I put my arm around you?"

"It feels funny. Like I wonder why you do it."

"I do it because I care about you. I think being hugged and kissed are two of the nicest things parents can do."

Katie winced. Her mind quickly thought of how Billy had kissed her. Suddenly a wave of nausea swept over her at the thought of Billy and what he had done to her. Katie felt sick when she remembered that night. She felt even worse knowing that she might now be pregnant. Mary's arm around her seemed even more uncomfortable.

Sensing how Katie felt, Mary removed her arm. "One of the things that you need to learn, Katie, is that love is a good thing. You look at my family and you think there's something wrong with us. The way we live, though, is the way normal people live. What we do just comes natural when everyone in the family has a healthy mind and feels good about themselves."

Mary thought it tragic that Katie truly didn't know what normal was. She thought to continue the conversation might be too much for Katie. Instead she changed the subject. "Would you like to look at some photos?"

"Of what?"

"My family." Mary rose and walked to a cabinet. She took out several photo albums. "This is sort of our history together." Once again she sat down next to Katie. Mary opened a dark green album. "This is when Donald and I were first married. Can you believe how thin I was? Goodness."

Katie looked at a very young Mary. "You were beautiful."

"And wasn't Donald a good looking man? He still is. His hair isn't as thick as it was back then, but he sure was a prize catch."

The wedding pictures made Katie feel sad. "I broke my mother's dishes. The ones she got when she got married. That was a real crappy thing to do."

Mary thought the best and said, "I'm sure it was an accident."

"I should have been more careful." Katie told Mary how the dishes became broken and how she later ran away.

Mary turned her head so that Katie wouldn't see the tears. "Like I said in the beginning, Katie. It was an accident. Your mother shouldn't have been so harsh to you."

"Would you have been angry with me?"

"No, Katie. I'd have been angry at myself for not fixing the shelf. I tell you, child, you just seem to look for ways to blame yourself for everything that happens in your life. You're just too hard on yourself." Mary knew it was again time to change the subject because they were drifting right back into things that were too personal. There had already been enough of that for one night.

Mary turned the pages of the album, commenting about her relatives and where the pictures were taken. "This is my son Malcolm. I had two boys by the time I was twenty-three. Both little sweethearts." Mary's fingers brushed across the page. "Just such sweethearts."

"Does Malcolm live here?"

A look of sadness crossed Mary's face. "No, child. Malcolm died two years ago. He was only sixteen. Just a child. He had leukemia."

"That's like cancer or something?"

"Yes. It's like cancer of the blood. He went through a great deal, and he was as brave as anyone could be. Strangely enough, Katie, he was the one who was sick, and yet he was the one who comforted all of us. We all loved him so much. We still do. There's not a day that goes by that I don't think about him." Tears filled Mary's eyes. She leaned her head into her hand and cried softly.

Katie sat silently for a few minutes. She wasn't sure what to say. Then she stretched her arms around Mary's shoulders and stroked her back. "I'm sorry, Mary. I'm really sorry that he died." As Katie sat there trying to comfort Mary, she suddenly realized that this was the first time she had ever put her arms around another person. Tears then began falling down Katie's face. Why, she wondered, did it feel so good to offer comfort to another? Why was there some sense that she was doing the right thing when she hugged Mary?

Later in the evening after Katie had washed up and put on her pajamas, she lay quietly in the bed and stared at the ceiling. Her mind could not stop questioning the fact that Mary's family seemed so much happier than her own family. What Katie could not decide was whether it was her family or Mary's family that was normal. Those things that passed between Mary, Donald, and Martin suddenly became things that Katie felt she would like to have.

As those thoughts passed through her mind, Katie turned her head and saw Mary standing in the doorway. "You ready for a good night's sleep?" Mary's shadow fell across the floor.

"Mary," Katie whispered. "I didn't mean your family was crazy."

Mary stepped closer to the bed. "Oh, honey, I understand. With some children they have to see normal before they know what it is. You haven't seen too much normal in your life."

Katie rolled over so that she could look at Mary standing over the bed. "I feel real close to you because you told me all about Malcolm. Like I guess I never thought that teachers cried or did the same stuff I do."

"Feelings are feelings, child. Everyone has them. Even teachers." She reached down and stroked Katie's head.

"I'm glad you let me come home with you. I really did like it."

"Would you like to come again sometime?"

"Yes, Mary. I'd like to come lots of times."

"Then we'll have to see what we can do about it. Now you get yourself to sleep. Tomorrow we're going to the zoo."

"My mom says that's where I ought to be kept."

"Well, your mom is wrong." Mary didn't like telling youngsters that their parents were wrong, but in this instance, she thought the words needed to be said.

Katie smiled and thanked Mary. "Mary." Katie called out her name softly. "Would you give me a hug goodnight?"

Mary wanted to smile but she felt too sad. "I surely will, child." She reached down and put her arms around Katie. She squeezed her and kissed her on the cheek. "Like I said, child, you get to sleep."

"Goodnight, Mary."

Katie rolled over and pulled the cover up under her neck. She could still feel the warmth of Mary's arms around her. Katie decided that before very long she would have to tell someone that she thought she was pregnant. There was a comforting sense in her knowing that Mary would be the one with whom she would share the secret.

CHAPTER EIGHT

Lucia walked into the office where Mary sat waiting. Mary could tell from the look on Lucia's face that the news was not good.

Mary asked, "It's true, isn't it?"

"Katie's a little over two months pregnant."

"Oh, Lord." Mary dropped her head to the desk. "We were making such good progress. We sure didn't need this."

Lucia flopped down in a chair and stretched out her legs. "Katie needs it even less. Do you have any suggestions?"

"They're not going to let her stay here. I know that."

"I know it, too."

"So many of the girls come here and they're pregnant. Sooner or later Lake Woods is going to have to set up a facility that will handle pregnant girls."

"That could get into a real can of worms." Lucia kept pulling at a strand of her hair. "Some of these girls have been using crack or they've downed too much liquor while they're pregnant. Lake Woods doesn't have the kind of money it takes to treat crack babies and the babies that are born drunk from their mothers' liquor. Darn. If some of these girls only realized what drugs and drinking are going to do to their babies."

"Some of them do, and they still don't care."

"What about Katie?"

"I'm sure she's telling the truth when she says she

never used drugs. What drinking she did, and she admits to doing plenty, was done before she got pregnant. We can hope. I suppose." Mary felt depressed in knowing that Katie would have to leave Lake Woods.

Lucia began tapping a pencil. "Someone is going to have to tell her parents."

"That's another 'Oh, Lord' story." Mary looked at Lucia who now bounced her shoe off and on her foot. "You look like a bundle of nerves today."

"I am. I just hate it when we can't help these kids." She stood up and paced around the room. "What are we here for, Mary? What are our jobs all about? Here we got this kid who's doing her darndest to get it together, and now we got to pitch her out."

"We're not going to *pitch* her out as you say. I'll work with her family on some solution."

"A solution with her family! You got to be kidding. They're going to go through the roof. They already think she's some kind of scum bag. I can just hear them raking Katie over the coals on this one. Has she been sick?"

"She throws up in the morning. Everyone has it figured out that she's pregnant. The superintendent asked me point blank if she were."

"What did you say?"

"What could I say? I said that you were taking her in to see a doctor today. Now I'm going to have to answer his question truthfully. He knows Katie is doing fine here. He's not happy about what's going to have to be done."

103

"What *is* going to have to be done?"

"I can tell you that I'm sure her parents are going to want her to have the baby. Then once the baby is here, the Bennetts will have *two* victims. They'll never shut up about it and get on with things.. They'll needle Katie until the day she dies, and I'd be willing to bet that as soon as that baby understands five words, they'll start in on the child."

"Mary," Lucia almost moaned the words, "it's going to be out of our hands. We have to face that. As nice as that kid is, we're not going to be making any final decisions about Katie."

"Then let's hope that we can teach Katie to make her own final decisions so that she comes out a winner."

"That's wishful thinking."

Mary barely whispered. "I know. I know."

Mary did what she knew had to be done. She told the superintendent that Katie was pregnant. Then she went to Katie's dorm to talk to her. The thing that Mary dreaded the most was telling Katie that she would have to tell her parents. Katie took the news much as Mary expected she would. She cried and pleaded with Mary not to tell her parents.

Mary put her arms around Katie and rocked her back and forth. "I wish it could be otherwise, but it can't. They have to know. You're a minor, Katie. That means your parents have the power to make decisions about your life."

Katie blew her nose and wiped at the tears. "I don't

know what to do, Mary. I don't want to be pregnant. I don't even want to think how I got pregnant. It was so horrible." Katie clenched her fists. "I hate him for doing this to me. I just hate him."

"It's good to say you're angry when you're angry. I'm glad that you can admit that you hate him. Are you going to tell your parents the truth about what happened?"

Katie shook her head. "They'll say it was my fault."

"Do *you* think it was your fault?"

"I shouldn't have let him do it. I should have screamed and woke up Gary. What did it matter if Billy left me there? They left me, anyhow, and now I'm still in this fix. Oh, Mary, I really don't want this baby. I just don't want to be pregnant."

Mary stroked Katie's hair. "I know, honey, but it might not work out that way for you. My feeling is that your parents are going to want you to have the baby."

"What am I going to tell them? They don't like me as it is. Now they're really going to hate me."

Although Mary strongly believed that everyone should face up to his or her problems if they hoped to find solutions, Mary felt that in Katie's case, maybe it would be better if an adult spoke in her behalf. "Let me handle it. Okay, Katie? I'll talk to them."

"My dad won't like you interfering. I told you he doesn't like black people."

"I just can't help who and what your father likes, Katie. Lucia and I are going to talk to him first." Mary took

105

Katie's face and held her chin. "Please dry your tears and trust us. We're going to do all that we can to help you."

On the following Saturday morning the Bennetts walked into the superintendent's office. Neither one of them had been told why they had been asked to come to Lake Woods. Mr. Bennett simply said that he had been expecting a call because he knew that sooner or later Katie would be causing trouble of some kind or another.

The presence of the tall superintendent seemed to have a settling affect on Bob Bennett. At least his presence had that affect until he told the Bennetts that Katie was pregnant. Bob Bennett then stood up and tossed his chair across the room. "That filthy, nasty girl. Wouldn't you know she'd let something like this happen to her. Just wouldn't you know it."

Lucy Bennett reached out to take his hand in an effort to calm him down. "Now it's not our fault, Bob, so don't be blaming yourself."

"Who's blaming me!" He shouted. "I'm not taking any blame for what that tramp did. Pregnant. Now isn't that just what this family needs. An illegitimate baby. I won't have it in my house. That's all there is to it. She's going to give that baby up for adoption because she's not bringing the thing to our house. Isn't that right, Lucy?"

If Lucy had disagreed, she never would have said so. "Whatever you think best, Bob. Just whatever you think best." Her concern was for him. Not one of her thoughts went to Katie. Lucy asked, "Then she can't stay here and have the baby?"

Mary answered her. "That's correct. We have no facilities here for pregnant girls. We could possibly make arrangements for her to go to a home for unwed mothers. There's one that's not too far away. Would you like for me to look into it?"

"No, I wouldn't." The last thing Bob wanted was to have the black woman involved in any way with his family. "I don't want any of you doing any more interfering in my life. I don't want Katie at any home for unwed mothers. Why the idea of her living with all those trashy tramps makes me sick. We'll make our own arrangements. Isn't that right, Lucy?"

Lucy folded her hands in her lap. "I think that's going to be the best way to handle it. That way we'll have some say-so about what happens."

That was what Mary feared the most. No matter how they handled Katie's pregnancy, Mary was sure their actions and decisions would benefit themselves far more than they would benefit Katie.

The superintendent looked at Katie's file. "I think we can manage to keep Katie here until the semester is over. There's no point in forcing her to quit in the middle of the semester. Her school work has been very good. I don't want her losing those credits. The additional few weeks also will give you more time to work out something. I hope your decision will be one that..." He looked at Bob Bennett and was at a loss for words. "Like I said, I hope the decision will be something that will help Katie."

Mary added what she knew was a useless point. "I'm sure we could arrange with the court to have some counseling for the entire family. Sometimes that helps in a situa..."

"Never mind any talk about counseling." Bob Bennett raised his voice. "Counseling is a bunch of garbage. If a man can't work out his family's problems, he's not much of a man."

Indeed, thought Mary. The sad part of the story, she concluded, was that in this case, the man of the family created most of the problems.

As the semester drew to an end, Katie felt terribly sad at having to leave Lake Woods. She felt even worse in knowing that she was going to be staying with fourteen nuns until the baby was born. Mr. Bennett had made arrangements to send Katie to St. Andrews, a home that was managed by nuns who did charitable work. In return for her room and board, Katie would help with the cooking and cleaning.

Katie rubbed her hands up and down the bulge in her stomach as she stood in Mary's kitchen. They both were waiting for one o'clock when Mary would drive Katie to St. Andrews.

Mary sat at the table, feeling as sad as Katie felt. "At least the place is in the city. Your parents will be able to come and see you. More importantly, at least I think so, is that Lucia and I will be able to visit you regularly."

The cup of tea that Mary had prepared for Katie grew

cold. "I know you and Lucia will come, but I doubt that my mom and dad will. Do you know they even lied to my sisters and brother about where I was? Dad said he was too ashamed of me to tell them that I was pregnant. Can you imagine being so ashamed that they don't even want me to talk to any of them until after the baby is born?"

"Where do they think you are?"

"At Lake Woods. Mom told them all that because I behaved so bad there that they were making me stay longer. Now my sisters and brother are going to hate me, too. I just can't get away from screwing up everything."

"Darn it!" Mary raised her voice. "Will you stop saying things like that? Your parents are far more to blame than you'll ever be. What is it with you, Katie, that you just can't like yourself?"

"What's there to like?"

"For a starter, you're a sweet girl. You're smart. You're a hard worker. There are all kinds of neat things about you. You're just so covered up with their criticism that you believe them instead of me. If I had sixteen years to work on your brain, I can assure you, you'd have a great opinion of yourself. That's what they've had, Katie. Sixteen years of hammering away at you to get you to believe that you're stupid and useless. That's not what parents should be doing to their children."

Katie leaned on Mary's shoulder. "I wish you could be my mother."

"I wish it, too, darling." Mary glanced at her watch.

"It's time. I'm afraid it's time to go."

Mary picked up the suitcase that she had bought Katie as a present. Both of them had laughed when Katie unwrapped the large going away present. Lucia had suggested it so that the next time Katie decided to run away, she would have a beautiful piece of luggage instead of a paper bag in which to keep her clothing.

The suitcase was placed in the trunk of the car. Katie climbed in the front seat. The trip to St. Andrews took no more than twenty-five minutes. As Mary turned up the driveway to the gates at the top of the hill, Katie stared out the window. "Heck, I didn't know all these kids would be here. I thought there would just be these old nuns walking around praying."

"This is an orphanage, Katie." Mary was upset with herself for not having explained more about St. Andrews. "You know what we should have done was visit the place before today. That way you would have felt more comfortable about coming. I'm sorry, Katie, that I didn't think of that."

Katie's eyes followed the children who were running and playing every place in the yard. "That's okay, Mary."

Mary glanced over at Katie. Her face seemed pleased with what she saw. "Does it make it better knowing there are little kids here?"

"In a way. I guess." There was pleasure in finding out that St. Andrews would not be a quiet place where she would be with older nuns all day. Almost instantly the pleasure faded when she saw a nun pushing an infant in a stroller. The waving hands of the baby reminded Katie why she was at St. Andrews, and that in the end, she would have to give her baby away.

Before Mary had even stopped the car, a young woman with cropped blond hair came quickly out the front door. She waved and smiled. "Hi. You must be Mary and Katie." The woman put her hand through the window of the car and patted Katie's arm. "I'm Sister Loretta."

Her warm smile and pretty freckled face made Katie feel at ease. She leaned over and whispered to Mary. "I thought nuns were ugly. She's beautiful."

Mary whispered back. "That's okay, darling. Your daddy thinks I'm from Africa." Mary opened the car door and took out Katie's suitcase. "Sister Loretta, this is my Katie. If I had brought you ten girls, together they wouldn't be as good a worker as Katie. She'll be a big help to you."

Loretta took the suitcase from Mary. "Welcome to St. Andrews, Katie. Have you been feeling okay?"

Katie shrugged. "I finally quit throwing up. Now my stomach is starting to stick out."

"Well, wait until you see Anita. You'll feel pretty tiny." Loretta linked her arm with Katie's.

Katie followed Loretta and Mary inside. The wax on the floors was so bright that Katie could see her reflection. "Who's Anita?"

"She's about your age. You're sixteen. Is that correct?"

"I just turned sixteen."

"So did Anita. She'll be with us until her baby is born. Anita is from Iowa. I know you'll like her. She was really looking forward to your arrival. Right now the only ones here who are expecting are you and Anita. Sometimes we have as many as five girls. We come to love them all." Loretta squeezed Katie's hand. Then she looked at Mary. "She'll be fine here, Mary. She really will. We do everything we can to make it as easy and pleasant as possible. Most of the girls come to think of us as this large collection of aunts who are hanging around waiting for the birth of their niece or nephew."

Mary had to do no more than look at Loretta's happy, beaming face to know that Katie could not be in better hands. "I can't tell you how relieved I am to know that Katie's going to be looked after so well. I was worried. Really worried."

"You just come here anytime you want, Mary. You'll always be welcome at St. Andrews. Now, Katie, let's just leave the suitcase here and I'll show you around. Anita works in the nursery school right now. Since she's grown so large this last month, we've pretty well kept her away from any kind of work requiring any pushing or pulling. Anita is very good with the children. We'll stop by there later.

"Now down this hall is the dining room and the kitchen. Because the sisters spend most of their time taking care of the children, we do have some hired help. Our hired help usually does janitorial work. Washing windows, mopping. Things like that. It used to be the sisters did every bit of the work. In fact, the older sisters are forever telling us younger ones how easy we have it compared to the work load they once carried. Do you get that from your parents, Katie? I mean how tough things used to be in the old days." Loretta grinned and opened the kitchen door.

Katie stepped inside the kitchen. On the other side of the room a young man was on his hands and knees working a scrub brush across the linoleum. He glanced up and stared at Katie. Quickly she backed out of the door. Her hand went to her throat as a wave of heat ran through her.

"What's the matter, Katie?" Mary came to stand beside her. "You look frightened or something."

Katie leaned against the wall. "My being here is not going to be a secret. Everyone is going to know."

"Why do you say that?" Loretta now stood with Mary and Katie.

"I know that boy."

"Rod?" Loretta asked. "How do you know him?"

"He's from my school. In fact, a long time ago I went to a dance with him. I even insulted him. He'll tell everyone at school. My sisters will find out. Then my parents will blame me. They'll think I told."

Mary tried to comfort Katie. "He might not even remember you."

"He'll remember me, all right. I told you I made fun of

him."

Loretta did what she could to assure Katie. "I'll talk to him. I'll make it clear that what happens at St. Andrews is a very private thing. He's an awfully nice boy. I think we can rely on him."

Katie peeked through the window in the kitchen door. Rod was still staring in the direction of the door. A frown spread across Katie's face. Reliable or not, Katie knew that Rod was a teenager like herself. That he would keep a secret did not seem like a reality to Katie.

CHAPTER NINE

By the sixth month of Katie's pregnancy her stomach still had not bulged out very much. Both Loretta and Mary thought the baby would be a girl because Katie remained so small. Katie argued that the child might possibly be a small boy, or perhaps, she laughed, a very thin boy. Katie thought more and more about the child she was carrying and the pain she would go through when she had to part with the child. On the one visit her parents had made to St. Andrews, they assured her that she could come home, but under no circumstances could she bring the child with her. Each night when she dozed off to sleep, Katie imagined herself going to the window of the nursery at the hospital and saying goodbye one last time to the child she had carried inside her for nine months.

She could see herself standing at the nursery window just as she had stood with Anita when the young girl came to wave goodbye to her daughter. Anita had named the baby Angela because she thought she looked like a little angel. Anita, like Katie, would be returning home. Her parents had also made it clear that there was no room and no money for yet one more baby in their household. Although Katie tried to comfort Anita, the girl was beyond comfort. She stared through the glass at the nursery and sobbed. Again and again she cried out to Angela that she would never forget her. That was a promise she would likely keep. The other promise, to come and get her as soon as she could take care of her could not be kept. Anita and her parents had signed the papers so that Angela could be adopted. In her heart, Anita knew that once the papers were signed, she would never see Angela again.

Anita's last words to Katie before she left the dorm were that Katie should not give up her baby. "No matter what, Katie, don't listen to them. Don't let them take your baby away."

Katie walked down the hall with Anita as she prepared to leave St. Andrews. "What can I do, Anita? I can't take care of a baby. My mom and dad won't let me bring the baby home."

Anita wrapped her arms around Katie's neck. "Find some way to do it, Katie. You just have to find a way. I'm hurting so much from giving up Angela. You just don't want to go through that kind of pain."

At night when Katie tried to sleep, she'd reach down and touch her stomach. The tiny flutter that rippled through her stomach to let her know that there was a life inside her, had turned to gentle thumps as the baby had grown and now moved stronger legs and arms. Katie thought so much about what Anita had told her, yet, she had no answers to her problem. In the end, Katie knew that she would have to do as Anita had done. The baby would be taken from her and she would be told about the wonderful life it would have with some couple who wanted the child more than anything in the world.

Giving up the child was a problem that lay ahead of her. One problem that was behind her was the fear that Rod would tell about her being pregnant and staying at St. Andrews. It was not long after he had seen her in the kitchen that he approached her in the common room where she was dusting. Katie had looked up and saw him standing near the door.

"Katie." He almost whispered her name. "Do you remember me?"

She started to answer him in a curt way as she had spoken to him in the past. Mary, though, had spent a great deal of effort to get Katie to see that she shouldn't talk to people the way her parents talked to her. As Mary said, there was no sense letting hateful and hurting things come out of her mouth as a means of defending herself when there was no need to protect herself.

Instead of answering sarcastically that, of course, she knew who he was, Katie smiled and said, "Yes, Rod. I remember you. We went to a dance together." She wanted to ask him if he had told anyone at school about her. Before she could ask, Rod volunteered an answer to the unasked question.

"Sister Loretta talked to me. She told me about your problem. I just wanted to let you know that I didn't tell anyone. I figure all this is your business."

"That was nice of you, Rod." Katie noticed that his clothes still looked shabby.

"I work here." He blushed and grinned. "You know that, of course. That was sort of dumb of me to say that."

"Don't feel bad. I win all the prizes for saying and

117

doing dumb things. Like this." Katie glanced down at her stomach. Then she, too, blushed. "It kind of couldn't be helped." Katie hoped that Sister Loretta had not told him everything, and she hoped he wouldn't ask.

Rod started moving backward out of the room. "Anyhow, I just wanted you to know that you don't need to worry about me. I'm not some kind of blabbermouth. I respect your feelings and your business."

Katie thanked him and went on dusting. As she ran the rag over the furniture, she thought how much nicer he spoke to her than any of the boys she had ever met. She couldn't imagine him being cruel like Billy or thoughtless and sloppy like Gary. Rod seemed more like Mary and Loretta. Caring and kind.

There were other opportunities for them to talk over the next few months. Rod came to St. Andrews one night a week after school and on the weekends. He never talked to Katie on the Wednesday night that he worked because he didn't believe in talking about personal things while he was being paid to work. When his cleaning chores were over, he had to dash out the door to catch the last bus to his neighborhood.

Most of the talking that he and Katie did was done on Sunday afternoons when Rod finished working at two o'clock. Their first meeting was by accident. Katie found herself heading out for a walk as he was leaving the kitchen. She walked him to the bus, and they talked for a few minutes. On that accidental meeting, Rod told her that maybe next Sunday he could take a walk with her because on Sunday he could catch a later bus.

The Sunday walks became something that Katie looked forward to doing. Katie learned that Rod would be graduating this year and that he had plans for going to a junior college. He wasn't sure what he wanted to be, but he thought of himself as fairly handy and that maybe he could become a shop teacher. Katie laughed and questioned him about whether he could stand being around teenage students all day. Rod stuffed his hands in his pockets and shrugged, answering that his own shop teacher seemed to like the students.

Most of what they talked about had to do with Rod's future. At first Katie found it difficult to talk about what she thought and felt because her future seemed so unsure. Then one afternoon Rod asked her about what she thought was ahead.

Katie frowned, fearing her own answer. "I just don't know, Rod. After the baby is born, I guess I'll just go home. My dad says I've had my last chance in school. I suppose I'll get a job or something like that. I don't mind working. I've always been a good worker. You are, too. I see how clean you keep the kitchen. Where did you learn to clean like that?"

"Oh, I've always helped my mom out. She works full-time. She's got enough to do."

"I never heard of a boy cleaning house. My dad and brother wouldn't pick up after themselves or clean the

119

house if the dirt was smothering them. What with all the girls we got in our family, the men don't do anything but bark out orders as to what they want and how fast we're supposed to move to get it for them."

"At our house it doesn't make any difference what sex you are. Like my mom always told us, if we live there, we're making a mess, and if we're making a mess, we got to help clean it up. It's not a problem. We all do our share."

Katie wondered if his house were like Mary's. A place where they didn't fight and argue. A home where everyone worked on solutions to problems. "You know, Rod, before I met Mary and saw how she lived, I probably would have thought your family was nuts. Now I'm beginning to wonder if it's not my family that's nuts."

"What do you mean?" Rod would have liked to have taken Katie's hand, but he just didn't think it was the right thing to do.

"All that yelling and screaming and hitting. Does that seem normal to you?" Katie glanced sideways at his pleasant face. She had long since stopped thinking how he dressed. Now she understood that he spent very little on clothes because he was trying to save for the future. A future that Katie envied.

Rod thought for a minute about what Katie said. Then he commented, "So many kids that I know come from all kinds of families. It's pretty hard to tell what normal is. I used to think that anyone who was rich was normal, but I'm telling you some of those rich kids at school are about as screwed up as anyone else."

"How do you think kids get to be normal? I'm beginning to think I'm not normal."

"Why do you say that?"

"Because look at me. I'm heading for seventeen and I'm pregnant and I'm living with nuns. Does that sound normal to you?"

He grinned and looked down at the path they were following. The last thing he wanted to do was to say anything that would hurt her. "You're going to be okay. Like you said, after the baby is born you can get a job. I always thought you were smart. You probably can get a good job."

"I'll tell you something, Rod, I'm smart enough to know you don't get a good job if you haven't even finished high school. I'm going to end up washing dishes some place or keeping house for someone. That's about all I seem to be trained for."

Rod stopped and took her hand. "Listen, Katie, don't start feeling all sorry for yourself. People who feel sorry for themselves usually don't get much sympathy from anyone else."

His remark angered her for a moment. "I'm not feeling sorry for myself. I just got a big mess ahead of me. I was just telling you how I felt. You don't need to be getting up and lecturing me or anything."

He raised his voice a little and showed his own disgust.

121

"Hang on, Katie. I'm not putting you down or anything like that. Sure you got a lot of stuff ahead of you. More than most girls your age have to deal with, but quit putting yourself down. It's like you say stupid stuff about yourself and then I'm never sure if you expect me to come back and say it isn't true, or if I'm supposed to agree with you."

Katie smiled at his predicament. "Yeah. I'm a real mess to deal with."

"See." He again raised his voice. "That's just what the heck I'm talking about. You're not a mess. You're just confused. Most of us are confused at some time or another. We got to learn how to work out the stuff. My mom says that's what you have to do if you ever want to grow up."

"You know what, Rod?"

"What?"

"I think Mary is right. I mean about what we learn. It sounds like your mom is real nice and teaches you good things. That's why you turned out so good. Now my nutty family learned from their nutty parents. Well, not nutty, as Mary corrects me. She says they came from troubled families. Mary thinks my family didn't learn how to handle things right. Then they taught me by their example. I'm talking about all that funny stuff. Like never hugging or kissing each other. And the yelling. You have no idea how tired I really get of that yelling. It's like no one ever speaks to each other. Yell and scream. Scream and yell. When the yelling and screaming doesn't work, they bad mouth each other or hit. Wham! Slap! That's how they think problems are solved."

A wave of pity raced through Rod for Katie. He couldn't imagine his mother hitting him for any reason. "It sounds terrible, Katie. I'm sorry you have to live like that."

"I got to learn, though, Rod. Mary says I got to learn other ways or I'm going to be just like them. Since I've been away from them for so long, I'm really beginning to see what they're like." Tears fell down her cheek. "Honest to God, Rod. I don't want to be like them. I really don't. I want to be a good mother. I don't want to hurt my kids."

He brushed his fingers down the side of her face. "I'll just bet you anything that you'll be a good mother, Katie. You're going to end up the best mother that a kid ever had."

From the time they had their first serious talk on that cloudy Sunday afternoon, Katie found it so much easier to tell him what she was thinking and feeling. What she had come to discover about Rod was that he did not judge her. When he thought she was wrong, he was honest and told her so. No longer did she pout or get upset when he told her what he thought. The thing she was learning from Rod was to talk things out, and that it was all right to have a difference of opinion. As he said, just because they didn't agree, didn't make either one of them wrong. It only meant that they didn't agree and that each of them could have an opinion.

As it grew closer to the time when Katie was supposed to have the baby, she realized how dependent she had

123

become on him. He, like Mary, had become someone she could trust. He was someone who was not going to say bad things about her or hurt her. Mary warned Katie that the hurt might come in that she had grown too attached to Rod. Mary reminded Katie that he was only a senior, and that to count on him for more than friendship would be unfair to him.

After Mary had been so honest with Katie, Katie forced herself to turn the fantasies into reality. The reality brought her pain. In her dreams she saw Rod marrying her and helping her raise her child. She found comfort in believing that Rod would protect her and that she would never have to go back to her mother and father. Such dreams began to fill her waking hours and she told Mary of her hopes. It was then that Mary gave her the warning. The warning included the reminder that Rod had plans for college, that he had responsibilities to his own family, and that he was far too young to take on all that was involved in marriage and raising a child.

Because Katie believed she could talk to Rod about anything, she told him that she cared about him, and that when she did her dreaming, he was a part of those dreams. "I just can't help it, Rod. You've been nicer to me than just about anyone except Mary."

At first Rod was at a loss for words. He knew that he had grown fond of Katie, but he also knew that he had his own hopes and dreams. He answered in a way that he thought would prevent his hurting Katie. "I've really gotten to like you, too, Katie. Sometimes I feel like I'd just like to take you in my arms and make everything okay for you. I know I can't do that, though. We sort of both have our own lives. Like we're both headed down a different path."

Katie leaned back against the step where they sat outside the chapel. "Yeah. I know that. I guess as long as I'm dreaming, I might as well dream good dreams. Who wants to dream bad dreams, anyhow?"

"You know I think part of it is that we can really talk. I mean like we're open with each other. I've never talked all that much to girls. I kind of like it." He smiled and patted her knee in an affectionate way. At this place you don't have anyone your age to talk with. I guess that's why you latched onto me. It's sort of like we both came along at the right time to help each other."

"Do you think we'll see each other after I leave here?"

"Probably." Rod hadn't thought much about whether he and Katie would keep up the friendship when she went home. "Between school, working here, and helping out at home, I don't have a lot of time. And this summer I'll be starting college. What can I say?" He looked at Katie to see if what he had said hurt her.

"Maybe we can just call each other once in a while. Just to sort of check and make sure we're okay. Do you think we could do that, Rod?"

"I don't see why not." Rod was mature enough to realize that Katie had come to depend on him, and it was a role he knew he could not live up to. "When you get a job and all, you'll probably be pretty busy yourself. You'll meet some nice guy where you work. Before I know it, when I call you, you'll say 'Rod? Rod who?' I just bet you."

Katie understood what he was trying to do. He wanted to paint a bright and happy future for her so that she wouldn't be thinking only of him. "Sure thing. The boss' son will fall madly in love with me. We'll get married and I'll live in a house with five bedrooms. Five bedrooms! Can you imagine that! Ugh. I hate to think about going back home and sleeping with my sisters. I hate to think about going back home and doing *anything*."

Rod reached down and pulled Katie up. "I got to get heading out for the bus." He put his arms around Katie. "You know I'm always going to care about you and what happens to you."

His kindness made her feel as if she were going to cry. "I know. And I thank you." She pressed her face against his. After so many years of not being held or hugged or touched, Katie rejoiced in finally discovering the joy of affection. It was impossible for her to imagine now what life would be like without love and tenderness.

Katie stood at the bus stop and waved goodbye to Rod. As she stared at the bus disappearing around the corner she wondered what her life would be like if she had stayed in school, and if she had stayed at the dance with Rod. She let out a deep sigh and wrapped her coat around her ever-growing stomach. Like Mary said, Katie thought, it was not good to dwell on the past. Life had to begin with today. Katie trudged up the path that took her back to St. Andrews. She felt sad and wasn't sure that she should think too much even about today.

CHAPTER TEN

When Katie's labor pains started, Mary phoned the Bennetts to tell them their grandchild was going to be born before too long. Bob Bennett was quick to correct her that the child was not *his* grandchild. And, no, he told Mary, neither he nor Lucy would be at the hospital for the birth. There was no sense, he told her, in creating any unnecessary pain for himself and for Lucy. He told Mary that they would be at St. Andrews when Katie was ready to come home.

The news did not surprise Katie. She had expected no less and no more from her parents. If there were anything to be grateful about, it was the fact that both Mary and Sister Loretta remained in the labor room with Katie, encouraging her to breathe and to push as the doctor had instructed them to do. Mary stood by the bed and held Katie's hand and stroked her head, repeating every few minutes that Katie was doing fine. One time Loretta came back into the room to tell her that Rod was in the waiting room.

Katie smiled. "That was pretty brave of him. Everyone is going to think that he's the father." She let out a low moan. "Is this going to be much longer? I just can't stand it anymore. Is it, Mary? Is it going to take forever for this baby to get here?"

Loretta wiped at Katie's face with a damp rag. She was more than familiar with how much difficulty teenage girls often had delivering their children. There was little point in thinking about how much better it would be if the young ones would wait a while before getting pregnant. "I don't think it will be much longer, Katie. You keep breathing those little puffs of air. That baby will be here before you know it."

Katie felt another contraction. She pushed and puffed. "Are they going to let me see the baby before they take it away?"

"Of course, Katie. Of course, you can see the baby." Loretta soothed her and kissed her fingers. Sooner or later Loretta knew she would have to tell Katie that she had a year to decide if she wanted to adopt the baby out. Loretta dreaded doing that because she had seen so much grief caused when some of the girls came back in six or twelve months to claim their babies. The parents who planned to adopt the infants had long since grown to love the babies. They thought of them as their own. They were the ones who had walked the floor with the children, and who had taken them in for their first shots, and who had sat up all night rocking them through their first illnesses. Then suddenly the natural mothers had a change of heart. They appeared on the scene, ill-prepared to take care of their babies. Yet the young mothers wanted their babies back. Of all the work that Loretta did, having to remove an infant from the home of those who had taken care of the baby during its first year of life was the hardest and most painful part of her job.

After twelve hours of waiting by Katie's bed as she

heaved back and forth trying to bring forth a life, Mary suddenly grabbed Loretta's arm. "I think this is going to be it."

As Mary spoke, the doctor came into the room. He smiled at Katie and wiped the perspiration from her forehead. "You about ready, young lady?"

Katie barely gasped, "I've been ready all day."

"Then let's see if we can't get this baby born."

Katie was wheeled into the delivery room. She wrapped her arms around her stomach, sure that the baby was going to come out any second. "I can feel the baby. I can feel it, doctor. It's going to come out."

What happened during the next thirty minutes was barely remembered by Katie. The thing that was imprinted on her brain was the sound of the baby crying. She laughed and looked up at the squalling infant covered with blood. "What is it?"

The doctor answered, "You just had yourself a little boy. A healthy little boy. We'll get that little guy's lungs cleared out, clean him up, and you'll be holding him in just a second."

Katie watched the nurse take the baby from the doctor. Her body blocked Katie's view, but she could hear his strong lungs calling out. "Are you sure he's okay and everything?"

"He's a fine one." The doctor stroked Katie's arm.

The nurse brought the baby to Katie. "Almost seven pounds. Six pounds and twelve ounces."

"Is that normal?" Katie asked as she peeked at the tiny face that turned beneath the blanket that the nurse had wrapped him in.

The nurse answered, "That's about as normal as you can get." She smiled and lay the baby in Katie's arms.

Katie first touched the baby's nose. Then she looked at his ears. Finally she wrapped his fingers around her finger. "He's so little. I just never knew babies were so little."

The nurse wheeled Katie back to her room. Mary and Loretta stood waiting in the hallway. "Congratulations!" Mary rushed to Katie, taking her hand. She and Loretta were dressed in the flowered gowns that the nurse had given them to protect the baby. They followed Katie into her room. "I can see his hair. He's darling. Oh, Katie, he's just so beautiful. You're going to love him to pieces." Suddenly the things that she said didn't seem right. They were true, but it bothered Mary that she was saying the things that one would say to a mother who was going to take her child home with her.

Katie craned her neck to get a better look at the baby. "I think I'll name him Michael. I always loved that name." Then she glanced at Loretta. "Will the people who adopt my baby keep the name that I give him? Michael John. That's what his name will be."

Loretta answered her truthfully. "Sometimes they do. I guess most of the time they do. I think it's a way of show-ing respect for the natural mother."

"I hope they'll call him Michael. I don't mean Mike. I

want them to call him Michael. That's his real name."
Katie was afraid to squeeze and hug him for fear he might break, but she wanted to hold him close.

The nurse came in and said that she would have to take the baby to the nursery. "We still have some things to do to check him out."

Katie pulled herself up on her elbows. "He's all right, isn't he?"

"Fine. Just fine. We do this with all the babies." She reached down and with great ease, scooped him into her arms, disappearing out of the room.

Immediately Katie felt a terrible sense of emptiness. She could only imagine what she would feel like when they took the baby for the final time. It was painful enough just seeing the nurse carry him away to the nursery down the hall. What, she wondered, would it be like when she had to stand at the nursery window as Anita had done, and say a goodbye that would last forever?

Mary bent down and kissed Katie on the cheek. "And how are you feeling, darling?"

Katie thought for a moment. "Happy and sad. You know, Mary, because I hate Billy so much because of what he did to me, I thought I wouldn't care about Michael. That didn't happen. I can't hate my baby. I love my baby."

"I know, sweetheart. I know." Mary looked up at Loretta. Both of them knew that the hardest part for Katie was still ahead of her.

For the next three days Katie remained in the hospital. She dreaded leaving because she feared she would never see Michael again. Every time the nurse brought the baby to her to be fed, Katie cried or sang to him. The doctor tried to assure Katie that some of the sadness was something that all new mothers went through. He called it *postpartum blues* and talked about the chemical changes that had taken place in Katie's body. Katie shrugged off his words. She was sure that the sadness she felt had nothing to do with chemicals. Her sadness, she believed, was in knowing that she would have to give up Michael.

On the third day as Katie put her few belongings into a suitcase, Loretta did what the law required her to do: She told Katie that she had one year to decide if she wanted to truly let Michael be adopted. Katie eased herself into a chair, careful of her tender stitches. "I wish you hadn't told me that."

"The law requires that I tell you."

They sat in silence for several minutes before Katie spoke. "In a year I'll be eighteen. Will that make any difference?"

"In what way?" Loretta could feel only sympathy for the young girl faced with such a difficult decision.

"Maybe I'll have a good job then. Maybe my mom and dad will change their minds. All kinds of things could happen."

"Don't give yourself false hope, Katie. No matter how you look at, it's very difficult being a single parent. Being one who has to worry about where the next bite of food is coming from, or if you and the baby will have a place to live, is a very heavy burden."

Tears ran down Katie's cheek. "But I love him."

"Sometimes loving a baby means doing the right thing for that baby. You have to ask yourself what the *right thing* is. What do you think it is, Katie?" Loretta felt she was being unfair to ask such a question of a girl who had just been through so much. There was nothing about her life that was in order. How could she make such a decision?

"I know Michael would have lots of good things with two parents. Especially parents who could buy him things and take care of him really good. But I love him. I just love him so much." Katie bent her head and sobbed. Her voice trembled as she spoke, "I just don't want to give him away. I'm never going to know what happened to him. For the rest of my life I'll wonder if he's happy. I'll probably even want to know if he's tall or if blue is his favorite color. Oh, Loretta." Katie leaned over into the nun's arms. "I just never thought this was going to be so hard. Never. Never!"

"Every time you think about Michael, Katie, you just think of him as smiling and laughing. In your heart you'll know that you did the right thing for him."

Loretta thought about the long talks that she had over the months with Mary. Both of them had tried to think of ways that Katie might be able to keep the baby, but both knew that she could not make it on her own with the infant, and that the Bennetts had made it clear again and again that the baby was not welcome at their home. Mary had even thought of how she might be able to take in Katie. To do that would have meant moving to a bigger place, and Mary knew that she could not ask her own family to sacrifice so much in behalf of a girl they barely knew. In the end, Mary and Loretta felt if Katie and the baby were to have any chance at life, the best thing for Katie to do was to give the baby up for adoption.

By the time Loretta and Katie had finished their talk, Mary had entered the room. She thought it best if both she and Loretta were with Katie when she said goodbye to Michael. None of them spoke as they slowly walked down the corridor toward the nursery. Several times Katie stopped and stood still, dreading her approach to the window that barred her from holding her baby.

"I'm so afraid. He's going to know I'm leaving him."

"No, Katie." Mary fought to keep from crying. "He's too young to know that."

Katie stood with her face pressed against the glass and looked at Michael's tiny fists waving weakly. His folded hand went to his mouth. "He's hungry. He does that when he wants to eat." Katie waved her hand. "Your mommy loves you, Michael. I really love you."

Mary put her arm around Katie's shoulder. "One day he'll know that, honey. That boy is going to grow up knowing that you loved him."

"Will the people who adopt him tell him about me?"

Loretta took Katie's hand. "I'm sure they will. We'll make sure they know all about you. We're also going to register you as the natural mother. Your name will be on file with the state. That way when Michael grows up and if he wants to find you, he'll know where to look."

"Do you think he'll ever want to do that?"

"Many children do," Loretta answered.

The three of them moved away from the glass. Katie felt faint. She felt the grief one would feel over a death. It was difficult for her to make one foot follow the other as she made her way down the hall and out of the hospital. The three days she spent in the hospital had seemed like years. On the ride back to St. Andrews, the three of them drove in silence. Not one of them believed there was anything they could say that could take away the sadness they all felt.

When Loretta turned the car up the gravel lane leading to St. Andrews, Rod flagged them down. He stood along the road. He stretched out his hand which held a bouquet of roses. "Welcome home, Katie."

The best that she could do was manage a weak smile. Home. This was not her home. "Thank you, Rod. That was real nice of you."

"I came to the hospital to see you, but because I wasn't a relative, they wouldn't let me in. Are you feeling okay, Katie?"

"Kind of weak."

"Will you be here on Sunday? Maybe we could take a walk."

Katie looked to Loretta. "Will I?"

"Your parents will be here on Sunday afternoon." She saw the disappointment in Katie's face. Loretta wasn't sure that she approved of the relationship that Rod and Katie had developed, but she knew he was a good boy and a good influence on Katie. "I think, though," Loretta smiled through the open window at Rod, "that we could make arrangements for you to have a paid holiday on Sunday morning. Does that meet with your approval, Rod?"

He grinned. "Thanks. Thanks a whole lot. That will be great." He realized that he had missed Katie while she was gone. More than that, he was fully aware that he had worried about her because he feared something might happen to her when she gave birth to the baby. "Is that okay with you, Katie? I mean like we'll take a walk Sunday morning before you leave?"

Katie squirmed in the seat from the discomfort of her stitches. "I'm not so sure about any long walk. Maybe a short sit?" She again tried to smile.

Katie went up to her room and lay down on the bed. Mary came to say goodbye and tell her that she would be back on Sunday to see her off. Katie turned her face into the pillow and sobbed. "Oh, Mary, you keep telling me all that stuff about living for today and planning about tomorrow. I hate today and tomorrow just stinks."

Mary sat down on the edge of the bed. "Things look

pretty horrible right now. You're still worn out from the delivery. Your emotions are just drained. When you get some of your strength back, you'll be able to think more clearly." Mary rubbed Katie's back. "Believe me, child, things will look better. They'll not only look better, they really will be better."

"What's going to be so much better?" Katie almost shouted at Mary. "Come Sunday I'll be leaving here and going back to all that screaming and yelling and hitting. My little Michael is going to be with two strangers who took him away from me. I got to say goodbye to Rod. You're not going to be my teacher anymore. I probably won't see Loretta anymore, either. Now, Mary, you just tell me what's so great about my life, and how I'm supposed to think good thoughts about today? I don't care anything about today. I really don't. I don't care about anything."

For all her years of living, Mary had no answers for her. "All I know, Katie, is none of us knows what's ahead for us. I do know, though, that what's ahead of us depends on what we learned from the past. You've learned a great deal about life. You've been through so much, darling. Now you put all that wisdom to use and make a better life for yourself. And don't you ever forget that I love you. No matter where you are and no matter what you're doing, I love you. You know that, don't you?"

Katie reached her arms up and hugged Mary. "I just wish you could promise me that everything will be okay."

138

"I'd be a fool to make a promise like that. It's not very often in life that *everything* is okay."

The next two days passed all too quickly for Katie. On Sunday morning she was up early and dressed long before it was time to meet Rod. When he walked through the gate at St. Andrews, Katie waved and walked toward him. Just as she wondered if she would ever see Mary again, she now wondered if Rod had been a person who had entered her life, added something to it, and now would disappear. She made the choice not to talk about anything serious today.

"Hi, Katie." Rod held out a small package. "I brought you a going home present."

Katie smiled at him. "You work real hard for your money. You shouldn't be spending it on me."

"Just say thanks like Mary taught you." He reached out to give her the wrapped package. "I got a card, too."

"Should I read the card or open the package first?"

"Suit yourself."

Katie opened the envelope and read the card. It was about friendships and how they never die or go away. She bit her lip and tried not to cry. "That's a real beautiful card. Thanks." Then she sat down on the bench in front of the flower bed that Rod often worked on. She opened the small package and found a locket. "Oh, Rod, it's gorgeous. I really mean it. It's the nicest present I ever got from anyone." She reached up to put it around her neck.

"Here. I'll help." Rod stood up and walked behind Katie. He brushed her hair aside and fastened the locket around her neck. "It looks great on you."

Katie's hand rubbed the smooth gold. "I'll keep it forever." Then Katie thought about what Mary had said about nothing lasting forever. "Mary told me that nothing lasts forever. I think she meant bad things The locket will last forever."

"I want you to think about me when you wear it."

"Then that will be all the time because I'm never going to take it off."

Rod and Katie were still sitting on the bench when Mary drove up the path leading to St. Andrews. She smiled and waved, thinking ahead to how sad it was going to be for her to say goodbye to Katie.

In the hour they had left the three of them talked about what Rod was going to study at college next summer, and about what types of jobs Katie should try to get. Mary had advice for both of them. She told Katie how she should dress for her job interviews, and what she should say to a would-be employer. "Be sure and tell them what a hard worker you are. Lord knows it's getting harder and harder to find good, hard workers. Once they hire you, darling, they'll realize what a jewel they have."

The time passed all too quickly. Mary glanced at her watch and reminded Katie that she needed to get her things ready as her parents would soon be there. Katie shuddered at the thought of their arrival. While Rod and Mary sat and talked, Katie went back to her room to get the suitcase that Mary had kindly given her. Loretta returned with Katie to where Rod and Mary sat waiting. No sooner had Loretta sat down when they all saw the Bennett's car turn up the driveway.

Katie felt so uneasy. "Well, I guess this is it." Her eyes filled with tears. "Boy, I better not let my dad see me crying. He thinks crying is pretty stupid."

Mary shot a glance at Loretta. More than anything, they both hoped that the time that Katie had spent away from her parents had been long enough for her to build some inner strengths so that she could deal with Bob and Lucy Bennett. "There's nothing wrong with crying, Katie." Mary took her hand. "Crying is an emotion like love. We need to let our emotions show."

"Not around my dad." Katie managed a weak wave to her parents, but the wave was not returned.

Mr. Bennett got out of the car and took Katie's suitcase. "I see you got yourself some fancy luggage to travel with."

"It was a gift from Mary."

"Feeling okay, are you?" He swung the suitcase into the trunk.

"I'm still a little weak."

He frowned. "Is that a complaint?"

Katie shook her head and looked at Mary. "Dad, this is Rod. He's a friend of mine. He works at St. Andrews."

Bob Bennett took Katie's arm and pulled her toward the car. "I'd say, young lady, after all the trouble that you caused us, the last thing we need to be hearing about is some other boy that you're interested in." He opened the door and motioned for Katie to get in. He merely nodded to the three of them who watched Katie being taken out of their lives. Then he turned around and thanked Loretta for taking care of Katie all these months.

As quickly as the car had entered the grounds of St. Andrews, it was gone. Katie leaned back in the seat. She waited for them to ask something—anything about the baby or about the birth. Neither said a word. "I named the baby Michael. He weighed nearly seven pounds."

Lucy turned around. "I know you been through a lot, Katie, but the sooner you forget all about the baby, the happier we'll all be. Now I don't want you to get in any habit of talking about any babies. Sooner or later you'll let something slip. Before you know it, the whole family will have wind of what you did. We don't want that kind of embarrassment. Do you understand?"

"Yes, ma'am." Katie remained silent She listened to them argue about everything from whether they had pan-cakes for breakfast last Sunday to what time Melba finished her homework the day before yesterday. Katie wanted to cover her ears to block out their voices. After just a few minutes Katie shouted, "Can't you two ever just talk about anything? Do you have to argue about *everything*?"

Bob Bennett stepped on the brakes. "Listen here, Katie, just who do you think you're talking to?" He turned around in the seat. "I hope those nuns haven't been putting any crazy ideas into your head. You just settle down. We'll tell you when we need to hear from you, and with no

142

more than what you got to say about anything, I can pretty well tell you, we won't be wanting to hear from you."

The engine hummed again as he pulled away from the curb. Katie pressed her head against the window and closed her eyes. Her mind thought: *They're not normal.* Again and again that same thought went through her head on the ride home. She sighed and fought back tears. Now that she knew what normal was, she questioned whether she could tolerate the madness of her own home.

CHAPTER ELEVEN

Despite Katie's pleas to be allowed to return to school, her father stood his ground. Again and again he told her that since she had given birth to a child, she was an adult now, and returning to school was out of the question. When Bobbie or her sisters asked why Katie was not going back to school, they simply were told to mind their own business.

Katie's business became that of finding a job. Lucy and Bob Bennett made it clear that she could not sit around the house all day and do nothing. Now that she was an adult, they expected her to earn a living and to help out with the expenses at home. Finding a job turned out to be much more difficult than Katie thought it would be. Day after day she filled out job applications. Always there was some feeling of shame when she had to put down that she had completed only three years of high school. Out of the more than sixty job applications that she filled out, only four businesses called her for an interview. All of them were fast-food chains, and Katie didn't want to work in a restaurant. She never told her parents about the interviews, or that one of the restaurants wanted to hire her. If they had known she had a chance to get a job and she had turned it down, they would have been furious with her.

Three months after Katie had come home from St. Andrews she was hired by a grocery store. For some reason that job appealed to her far more than frying hamburgers. She went to a training school to learn how to bag groceries properly. It was a task that she was very good at doing because she moved so quickly and efficiently. The clerks who rang up the groceries certainly noticed that Katie was among the best of the baggers.

Katie's hands flew as she passed the groceries from her left hand to her right hand and directly into the bags. It seemed like but a few minutes before she had the largest purchases bagged and in the carts. Mr. Boswell, the store manager, was not one to miss noticing when he had a good worker on his hands. He complimented Katie by telling her that he thought she was the best worker that he had hired in a long time. His compliments only drove her to work all the harder and faster. He told Katie that he was sure when the next position for a checker opened up, he was going to recommend her for the job.

At dinner that night Katie waited for a chance to tell her parents the good news. As usual, the other children argued about everything from whose turn it was to dry the silverware to who had left a towel in the bathroom last night. While the children yelled back and forth at each other, Lucy and Bob never stopped commenting how they wished they had never had so many children. Lucy dwelled on how much it cost them to raise the children, and Bob hammered away at how there was never any peace and quiet in the house because of the children. The thing he said he most looked forward to was the day when they'd all be gone.

Katie thought his last remark provided her with an

opportunity to say what she wanted to say. "You know I'm getting a promotion."

"So." Lucy looked up at her. "What's that supposed to mean?"

"I'll make more money as a checker. I might be thinking about getting my own place. Marjorie at work was talking to me about sharing an apartment when I get a checker's job."

"Now hold on there." Bob pointed his fork at her. "You're not going any place. The very idea of you moving out from under this roof is about the most stupid thing I've heard this year."

Lucy added, "Don't be getting any grand ideas about yourself, Katie. If you get any raise, you can just add to the room and board you're now paying. We put out our good money all these years to keep you fed and clothed and to buy you everything you wanted. Now it's about time you started paying us back."

"But I thought you just said you couldn't wait for us to move out. I talk about moving out, and you jump all over my case."

Bob took another bite of meat. "You don't have any case. As long as you live in this house, what you have is our rules. Take them or leave them."

As usual, Katie was baffled by their conflicting messages. Take the rules or leave them. That could mean obey her parents or get out. Yet they forbid her to leave. Her father commented that he couldn't wait for them to be gone, yet, the mere mention of her leaving made him angry. Katie wondered if she would ever understand what it was they expected of her.

Rather than continue talking about leaving, Katie made an effort to let them know that she was well liked at work, and that Mr. Boswell thought she was among the best workers at the store. "I'm really doing great at work." She waited for some response from her parents. There was none. "Mr. Boswell said that I bagged groceries faster than any other bagger."

Lucy finally commented. "That's because you're probably doing it wrong. I bet that Boswell gets complaints about you all the time. He's probably too polite to say anything."

Katie felt a knot in her stomach. The ache came from the resentment and anger raging through her. To speak up would only lead to more trouble and more arguments. To remain silent made her feel physically ill. Again and again she repeated to herself as she tried to eat, *They are not going to make me feel ashamed of myself.*

"And another thing, young lady," Bob Bennett again pointed his fork at her, "you better not be counting on that raise until you get it. By the time that so-called promotion comes due, your manager is going to wise up about you."

"What do you mean by that?" Katie asked.

"That you'll never get those groceries rung up right. You'll have that whole store in a mess before the day is over."

Katie's fists came crashing against the table. "That's not true. What's wrong with you, Dad? Why can't you ever say anything good about me? Other people think I'm okay. You and mom just aren't happy unless you're bad mouthing me. I'm sick of it. Just plain sick of it."

Bob pushed his chair back and rose to stand over Katie. "You better be thinking about what you're saying, Katie. You better not dare cross me. You hear what I'm saying?" His face turned red with anger.

Lucy's voice rose above his. "Bob, you sit yourself down. There's no sense getting yourself all riled up over *this* child. She's just getting too fresh for her own good."

Katie's sisters looked back and forth from her to their parents. Each waited with a certain amount of eagerness to see what was going to happen. Bobbie moved closer to Katie as he feared her defending herself was really going to send his father into a rage.

Katie pushed her own chair back and walked around to the other side of the table. Feeling safer at having put distance between herself and her father, she warned, "You're not going to hit me anymore, Dad. No more. I'm an adult now."

"You're no adult. You're a punk kid. And you better get yourself straightened out."

"You were the one who said I couldn't go back to school because I was an adult. If I was an adult for that reason, then I'm an adult now."

"I've had it with you, Katie." He picked up a plate and

threw it at her.

Katie backed up toward the living room. Her pulse pounded and the room seemed to be spinning as her defiance grew. "You can't settle problems by throwing dishes, Dad. You can't find answers when everyone is screaming and yelling. Normal people talk. Normal people don't hit each other. This family is crazy. That's why we fight and argue and throw plates at each other. We're all crazy."

"You're the one who's crazy, Katie. You've got this whole family torn up. Look at your brother and sisters. Do you see them acting the way you do?"

Katie stared at their faces as they sat astounded by her challenges to their father. Katie looked from one to the other, and said, "Well, you better learn that this family is crazy and you better start doing something to help yourselves, or you're going to end up just like mom and dad."

Bob Bennett screamed, "And what's wrong with us?" He tried to move closer to her. He wanted to strike her, but she kept safely out of his reach.

"You're rotten parents is what's wrong with you. You don't know anything about how to show love. You don't have a clue how you're supposed to help and encourage your own children. All you've ever done is tell me what's wrong with me. I'm surprised I'm not as nutty as you are. I'm me, Dad. You never loved me just because I'm me."

"So what are you, Katie? You're a filthy tramp. Just look what you let happen to you. Now you try to tell me you're decent when you're really just a nasty, filthy girl."

149

Tears fell down her face. He had struck at the thing that hurt her the most. Not a day went by when she didn't think of Michael. Michael, she believed, was something good that had happened to her. Now her father made it seem that his birth was something dirty. Katie turned and ran from the room. No matter how much she fought back, she felt her father was so much stronger and that he would always win.

The next day when she finished working, Katie called Mary and asked if she could come by and see her. Mary understood without Katie having to say anything that there must have been another battle at the Bennett house. Over the last few months, every time Katie felt burdened down by her own family, she would find comfort with Mary.

When Katie arrived, Donald was in the kitchen, as usual. Katie could smell the fried chicken that he was preparing. "I could smell that chicken when I was coming up the walk. Donald ought to open up a restaurant."

"Katie. Katie. Katie." Mary threw her arms around the girl. "You're getting so thin, child. Aren't you eating right?"

"It's bagging all those groceries. I burn up about a million calories a day." Katie couldn't wait to tell her about the promotion. "You know what, Mary?"

"I can tell by the glimmer in your eyes that it's good news."

"Mr. Boswell is going to promote me."

"Well that just shows what a smart man that Mr.

Boswell is." Mary called to Donald. "Honey, did you hear what Katie said? She's getting a promotion."

"Hold on. I want to hear all about it." Wearing a big grin, Donald came into the living room and kissed Katie. "You say you're getting a promotion, Katie? Well, how about that. Why you haven't been there any time at all, and already they're promoting you. Isn't that something? I tell you, girl, we're proud of you."

Katie blushed and thanked him. It was impossible for her not to compare their excited reaction to the criticism of her own mother and father. All through dinner Mary and Donald asked Katie a dozen questions about her job and what she liked about it. By the time the meal was over, Katie believed that her job had to be one of the most impor-tant jobs in the whole world.

While she and Mary cleaned up the kitchen, Katie brought up the subject of her moving out and being on her own. "Oh, Mary, you should have seen him! He just raged at me. Do you think I'm crazy for wanting to do that?"

Mary thought for a minute. Ever since Katie had been at St. Andrews she had matured way beyond her years, but having just turned seventeen made Mary wonder if Katie truly were old enough to be by herself and to have the responsibility of seeing that all her bills were paid.

"Well?" Katie pressed for an answer.

"I'm thinking, child. My brain is working overtime on this one. Seventeen is pretty young to be making so many decisions and having to worry about whether you have the money for rent, or utilities, or food. Do you think it might be better to save a little? Perhaps enough so that you have several months rent?"

"How can I save?" Katie wiped the dishes and placed them on the shelves. "I have to give them almost everything I make. I'll never get any money in the bank. Besides, I'll be splitting all the bills with Marjorie."

"Tell me about Marjorie." Mary was curious about the young woman who had offered to share an apartment with Katie.

"Well, she's twenty-four. She's been at the store since she was just a little over twenty. Marjorie told me I need to be thinking ahead about some kind of career. She thinks it's terrible how the stores treat us."

"What do you mean?"

"They only hire part-time workers so they don't have to pay us as much and there aren't that many benefits. Marjorie thinks the unions ought to get stronger. She says I ought to join the union when I get to be a checker. Anyhow, she told me there's not much future for me at the store. I need an education is what she said."

Mary grinned. "I think I like this Marjorie."

"Yeah. She's been a real help to me. You know what Mary?"

"What child?"

"I told Marjorie about Michael. The same thing happened to her. I guess that's why she understands about me. I mean I suppose that's why she's been so nice and all. She said I shouldn't be rushing into marriage or anything like that. Marjorie finally married the guy who fathered her child. That was *after* he wanted her to give the baby up for adoption. Marjorie said she was miserable with him. He was always hitting on her and other terrible stuff. She was so sad at having to give up her baby. Then she got pregnant again and he wanted her to get rid of that baby. Marjorie wouldn't do it. She had the baby and she kept him. His name is Todd. He'd live with us and I could help her take care of him."

"Oh, I see." Mary nodded. "And you don't suppose living with Marjorie might have some appeal because she has a young son? A little boy that might help to fill up some of the void that you still feel because of Michael."

Katie put the last of the dishes away. "You know, Mary, I thought about that very thing." Katie stared out the window as she talked. "But you know what I remembered?"

"What, darling, did you remember?"

Katie took Mary's hand. "You see, I'm always remembering things that you tell me. I remember when you told me that no one could ever replace your son who died. He had a special place in your heart, and that was his place. You said that you would always remember him for who he was, and that if you had ten children, not one of them could fill the void that was made when he died. That's what I thought about. I have a place in my heart for Michael and I'll never forget him. Helping take care of Todd isn't going to make me miss Michael any less or make me stop wondering how he's doing."

Mary reached over and kissed Katie on the cheek. "You know I've met people who are supposed to be adults, and they aren't nearly as smart as you are, Katie. You truly think things through."

"And wasn't that nice of you to say that!" Katie laughed.

They went into the living room and sat down to talk again. Once more Katie asked about living with Marjorie. Mary answered her by saying that the decision had to be her own. "We can talk about it, honey. Maybe I can bring up some ideas that you hadn't thought about, but the thing about life is that when it gets down to the final decisions, we usually have to make them on our own."

"I'm going to think about it some more, but I sort of think I have my mind made up. And another thing, Mary, I been thinking about going back to school. Maybe night school. How long do you think it would take me to finish school if I went at night?"

"I know several of the high schools offer GED programs at night. Is that what you had in mind?"

"Since I work days, it would have to be at night. I mentioned it to mom and she said with my brain, I'd have to go to school day *and* night if I ever wanted to graduate. She's something else, isn't she?"

Mary closed her eyes and leaned back in the chair. "I'm not defending your mother, Katie. I know how difficult she and your father can be, but I'm sure Lucy can't help the way she is. I mean she could help her ways if she could ever figure out that she's doing some very wrong things. You have to know what you're doing wrong before you can begin to change. And you can't change unless you want to change. She's locked into raising you children the same way she was raised. And Lord knows, her parents were probably raised the same way they raised her. It usually goes back for generations. They just keep passing on all the bad stuff. You, though," Mary reached out to touch Katie's hand, "are going to break the cycle. As young as you are, sweetie, you can see that it's not a good way to raise children."

"Raising children sounds terribly scary." Katie stood up to leave.

"Would you like for me to find out something about the GED classes?"

Katie stretched her arms around Mary's neck and hugged her. "Thanks for offering, Mary. I'm the one who wants to go, so I better be figuring out how to go about doing it."

Mary grinned as she waved goodbye to Katie. There was a spunk and a bravery to the young girl that made Mary realize that Katie would succeed in life. No matter how much her parents had insulted and belittled her, and no matter how many times they had hit her, Katie had kept her spirit. Yes, Mary, thought, Katie would make it.

CHAPTER TWELVE

It was one of those rare Saturday nights when Rod had a little free time. He had written his term paper for his first English course at college, and he felt the need to relax. As usual, he looked forward to meeting with Katie. She would not let him come to her house, so he met her near the movie theater in the downtown area. Their plans were to eat and go to the show. Since Katie had been given her promotion, she wanted to treat Rod to a dinner and a movie.

Rod was very excited for her and the raise she received. "Aren't you proud of yourself?" He took her hand and squeezed it.

"You're darn right I am." Because her parents showed no pride in her raise and promotion, Katie had made up her mind to simply feel good about her own accomplishments whether or not her parents gave their approval. "It was really scary at first. It's not so bad when the computer light picks up the prices. What makes me nervous is when I have to check the prices out on the cost sheet. That really slows me down."

"You're probably still faster than the rest of them."

"Thanks for thinking good things about me."

"You're welcome." Rod opened the menu and stared at the list of foods. "What are you going to have?"

"I don't know why I even look. I always get a ham sandwich, fries, and a malt."

"You ought to eat some vegetables once in a while. You look thin."

"Mary's always saying the same thing. I thought boys liked thin girls."

"There's a difference between being skinny and being thin. You're getting downright skinny." He glanced up to see if he had hurt her feelings with the truth.

Katie just smiled and said that she'd order a salad to please him.

"Don't eat to please me. You order what you want."

When the food came Katie began with the malt. "How's school going?"

"Whew." He pretended as if he were wiping perspiration from his forehead. "College is not like high school. I can tell you that for sure. I read more in a night than I did all week when I was in high school."

That news didn't set well with Katie. They saw each other so seldom, and when they did, he always mentioned how busy he was. His words gave her very little hope that she would get to see him any more often than she was now seeing him. She wondered if he had any idea how much she had come to care about him.

"What's going on with you? I mean at school."

"It's really too early to tell. I only just started. I'm the youngest one in the class. You know, Rod, there's a sixty-two-year-old woman in my class. When the teacher asked us why we wanted to work on a high school diploma, this old lady said that she was going to graduate from high school before she died, and it didn't matter how long it took her."

Rod laughed. "That sounds like something my mother would say. She's real determined. Like you, my Katie."

She loved it when he said *my Katie*. It made her feel as if she belonged to him. "So, anyhow, I got my books and all. I swear, though, I have to argue with my dad every time I go out the door. He says going is stupid and a waste of time. Sometimes I wonder if there's anything in his life that he doesn't think is stupid."

"Have you and Marjorie made any more plans?"

"Marjorie keeps looking for something that she can afford on her own just in case I can't move in with her."

"Have you given up on that idea?"

"Not completely." Katie lifted up the bread on her sandwich. "Hand me the mustard, please." She dribbled thin ribbons of mustard across the ham. "I really don't know what to do. My dad has the law on his side. I'm still a minor. He could make me stay at home. Knowing him, he'd probably have me arrested if I moved out. I'd hate for Marjorie to count on me, and then let her down. I think I'll just see how the job goes and if I can handle it. When I'm sure Mr. Boswell is going to keep me as a checker, I'll probably talk to Marjorie again. Oh, Rod, you should see Todd. He's so darling." Her eyes grew misty and her voice trembled thinking about Marjorie's little boy. "He just does the cutest things."

Rod set his sandwich down and took her hand. "You're thinking about Michael, aren't you?"

"I always think about him. He's probably crawling by

158

now. Maybe even standing up. Mary's right, of course. I'll think about him until the day I die." Katie wiped at her eyes with the napkin. "I'm sorry. Tonight was supposed to be fun, and here I am slobbering all over the place and sitting here with my nose running. I'm a real glamour puss, huh?" She blew her nose.

"Come on and finish your sandwich. That movie is supposed to be pretty funny. It sounds like you could do with some funny stuff in your life."

Katie took the last bite of her salad. "See. My plate is all clean. Are you proud of me?"

"I'll always be proud of you. Are you sure you want to pay for all this?"

"Listen, I'm a big important checker now. I'm rolling in money." Katie opened her wallet. "Do you think three dollars is a big enough tip?"

"Sounds about right to me." Rod took Katie's hand as she pushed up from the chair.

"Such a gentleman." She wrinkled her nose and smiled at him.

Rod was correct about the movie. Katie found herself laughing. In the dark theater she also found it was possible to forget about her problems and to think about nothing except the movie. That was possible only until Rod reached his arm around her and rested it on her shoulder. Katie no longer felt uncomfortable whenever anyone touched her. Through Mary and the sisters at St. Andrews, Katie had learned that wanting affection was a very normal feeling for all people. What bothered her about Rod putting his arm around her was that it only made her more aware how much she cared about him. With his hand resting on her shoulder, she realized it was difficult to concentrate on the movie. Deliberately she moved her face closer to his until her forehead rested against his chin.

Rod sat more rigid as Katie moved closer. Now he was the one who felt uncomfortable at her closeness. Instead of brushing his face against her forehead as Katie hoped he would do, Rod removed his arm and said that he was going to get some popcorn. When he returned, he didn't put his arm around her again. His lack of attention made Katie feel uneasy. The first thing she did was ask herself what she had done wrong. As the story on the screen came to an end, she had no answers. When the movie was over, Katie walked in front of Rod up the aisle. Once or twice she could feel his hand on her back as he guided her toward the exit. His touch made her question again what she had done to make him not want to put his arm around her.

After the show Katie glanced at the clock in the lobby. "It doesn't look like we have any time left." Her voice betrayed how sad she felt. "Having a job and earning my own money doesn't seem to make any difference about curfews. I still have to be home by ten-thirty. Now instead of his saying *school nights*, he talks about *the night before I got to get up and go to work*. Ick."

Rod started to reach for her hand. Then he pulled back and put both of his hands in his pockets. "So do you think we better head for the bus stop?"

"Probably." Katie felt her stomach churning. There were so many things that she wanted to ask him and to tell him, but they had no time. It might be a week, even two weeks, before she saw him again. She knew that during that time she would not only miss him, but she would wonder over and over again if he liked her, and if he wanted to be around her. In the past it never seemed to matter what he said. Because Katie constantly had to fight for her self-esteem, she often could not believe that anyone as nice as Rod could like her despite his assurance that he did.

Several people waited at the bus stop. Katie pulled back away from them. "I hate standing so close. They can hear everything you say."

"Yeah," Rod grinned, "but we can hear everything they say, too."

"Who would want to?"

"Aw, sometimes it's kind of interesting listening in on conversations. It's fun trying to figure out who they're talking about, or what happened to them before they started the conversation. People are really strange. Interesting, but strange."

"Do you think I'm strange?"

"Come on, Katie, why do you ask something like that?"

"Oh, I don't know. I just feel weird sometimes.

"Why?"

"Because I don't quite fit in. I sure don't fit in with my

161

family anymore. Thank god for that!" Katie shook her head and looked upward. "I'm the youngest one at work. Except for Marjorie, I don't have much in common with the other people. I can tell school is going to be like that, too. Those people are all in their twenties except for that sixty-two-year-old lady. Girls my age seem so silly. Like they're not as grown up as me. Where do I fit in, Rod? It's depressing."

Rod quickly asked about the thing that bothered him so much in the past. "You're not drinking again, are you, Katie?"

"For crying out loud, Rod, I quit that dumb stuff. That's the last thing I need is one more problem. I could have become some kind of alcoholic or something. Who needs that."

"You've come through a lot in the last year, Katie. A lot more than most kids get through. It's okay to get down once in a while, but things look like they might be working out for you. Do you get depressed very much?" He still worried about her trying to escape life's problems by turning to liquor.

"I just want to fit in and feel like I belong some place." Katie looked directly at him. "And I don't want to just belong some place, I want to belong to someone." She emphasized the *someone*. Katie wasn't sure how she could make it any clearer to him how she felt.

Rod watched the people boarding the bus. "You better get in line or you'll miss the bus." She had brought up a subject that made him feel uneasy.

Katie shook her head. "I'll catch the next one."

"You won't make it home by ten-thirty."

She leaned her head against the brick building. "I don't even care."

"You'll get in trouble."

"I'm always in trouble, anyhow."

The bus pulled away from the curb and they stood in silence for a moment. Then Rod felt that he had to say what needed to be said. "You know, Katie, I really do care about you."

"Sure. I know that." Katie wasn't sure if she wanted to hear what she thought he was going to say. "Are you trying to get up the courage to tell me you're going to dump me?"

"For crying out loud, Katie." He walked in a small circle to relieve the stress that he felt. "You don't *dump* your friends. You're the best friend I got."

She didn't want to ask, but she did. "Is that all I am to you? A friend?" Her hopes over the last few months had been for so much more.

"No. You're a lot more than that."

"Well, then, what am I to you? Am I a girlfriend? Just tell me what it is I am. I really don't know."

"You know I don't date anyone else if that's what you mean."

"That's because you're too busy. You wouldn't have time to be running the streets with cute girls in short skirts."

Katie tried to joke with him, but her voice sounded serious.

"We're just so young, Katie."

"Too young to belong to each other?" She silently prayed that he would deny what she just said.

"I think we sort of belong to each other."

"Then how come you never told me that you love me?"

"Katie, at eighteen I got school ahead of me for another four years. If we start talking about belonging to each other and loving each other and all that serious stuff, neither one of us is going to do some of the things we want to do."

"There's nothing I want to do." Katie wondered what he meant.

"Sure there is. You want to get your GED. You want to get a better job and get yourself set up some place so that you're on your own. That's going to take time and plenty of hard work." Rod scraped the toe of his shoe along the sidewalk. "Maybe I don't know what you want from me, Katie, when you talk about all that belonging stuff."

Katie waited a long time before answering. Her thoughts went back to some of the conversations that she and Mary had. Again and again Katie had come to realize how important it was for her to feel loved and to have the affection and praise that had been denied her for so long by her parents. Mary had told Katie that when children didn't feel loved and didn't get the affection that all children need, many children went in search of both. Mary believed that many deprived and abused children eventually chose to give up and withdraw or they became very angry. Other children kept up the search, always looking for the person who could give them what they had missed out on as young children. Mary warned Katie that it was unfair to try to get anyone to make up for the neglected years.

As Katie looked at Rod pacing about in circles, she couldn't help but think that maybe she was wanting and hoping that he could give her the love and praise that had so far escaped her. She wanted to answer his question about what she wanted from him, but she wasn't sure what to say. In reality, Katie didn't know what *belonging to someone* meant. "I get all mixed up, Rod. I guess I just say a whole bunch of words and I don't even know what I'm talking about."

He reached for her hand and stroked it. "I'm mixed up plenty of times myself. Like now." He put his arms around her. "I know I care about you, Katie. I like to hold you. More than anything I'd like to kiss you."

"Oh, Rod. I guess that's what I mean. I love to hear those things. I just would love to know that you feel that way about me and that we could always be together."

His hold on her became more gentle. "And that's what I mean, Katie. We're too young to be talking about always being together. Neither one of us has a clue where we're going in life."

"Can't we figure that out together? I mean you and me will always look out for each other and..." Katie was unable to think what else should be in their plans. Simply looking out for each other seemed enough for her right now.

"Katie, I've told you I care about you. For now we have to settle for seeing each other once in a while. I don't want to go around making any big promises about us. Why can't we just see each other and talk and have some fun? Well, I don't mean just have fun like most kids our age. I mean we can let each other know we care and go to the show and things like that. Honest to god, Katie, I can't do much more than that. I honestly can't."

"All I know, Rod, is that I'd rather see you every two weeks than see some other goofy creep every night of the week." She rested her head on his shoulder. Then she lifted her mouth toward his. "Would you kiss me?"

Rod's hand went up to her face and he gently stroked her cheek. Then he leaned over and kissed her softly on the mouth.

Katie drew back after he pulled his mouth away from her lips. "I sure haven't kissed many guys, but I'm positive that wasn't much of a kiss."

His disappointment showed on his face. "I guess that's the best we ought to try for."

"If you loved me, you wouldn't think like that. You'd want to kiss me really serious like. Donald gives me better kisses than that." Katie was close to pouting.

Rod patted Katie on the top of the head. "Listen, I'm smart enough to know that if we start getting serious about kissing, we're headed for trouble. Haven't you had enough trouble already in your life?"

166

His words hurt. "You mean Michael. You're saying that because of kissing and what it lead to that I had Michael. That I was a tramp like my dad says. Oh, Rod, I didn't expect you to think things like that too." Katie pulled away from him.

He raised his voice so that even the people waiting for the bus turned around to look at them. "I never said any such thing, Katie. You're twisting this all around. All I meant was you and me should cool it. Hold hands or I can put my arm around you. I don't want anything to go any farther than that." Rod reached out to hold her arms. "We don't need to be having babies, Katie. We need to be getting our lives figured out."

What he said to her was ignored. Katie was hearing only what she wanted to hear, and she was confused about what Rod meant. "Well, you won't have to worry about that." She yanked her arms free of him. "I'm better off just not loving anyone. You see what loving someone does? More fighting. That's just what I need in my life is more fighting."

"We're not fighting." Rod tried to control his voice and his feelings. "I'm trying to talk to you. There's a difference between fighting and talking. We're talking."

"No we're not." Katie could feel only anger. Once again she believed that Rod was saying that getting pregnant was her fault, and now he wanted no part in any feelings that might lead her to becoming to pregnant again. "I got to go. If I miss that bus, I'm really going to get it."

"Katie, please. I don't want to argue."

"Then quit saying things like you said and maybe we won't argue."

"If we're going to be friends, I have to be able to say what I'm thinking without you getting all mad."

"You know what, Rod? I don't want to know what you're thinking. It sounds like you're thinking like my dad. I sure don't need any more of that kind of stuff in my life."

"Katie, you just got everything screwed up. All I said was we care about each other and we need to be careful about what we get ourselves into. You're making it sound like I called you some dirty name, or that I said something bad about you. It hurts my feelings that you'd think something like that."

Her own feelings mattered more to her at that moment. He had never said that he loved her. He didn't want to kiss her as a young man his age would want to do with someone he cared about. And, finally, Katie believed that Rod had brought up the pregnancy and Michael to hurt her. All she wanted to do was to get away from him. She darted free of him and ran for the bus without so much as saying goodbye.

On the ride to her street, Katie sat huddled in the last seat on the bus. Tears ran down her face. She leaned over and asked a woman if she had a tissue that she could have. Katie took the tissue that the woman silently offered. Then she blew her nose and knew that she had to stop crying because she could not ask the woman for another tissue.

Katie wrapped her arms around her middle, and sat huddled in the back of the bus. After the crying stopped, she felt numb. All that she had expected of Rod was that he hold her and that he love her. Katie lowered her head into the palms of her hands. Rod, she quietly cried to herself, was like her parents. He could not give her what she needed, and that thought filled her with fear for her future.

Katie stepped off the bus and walked the three blocks to the small house she had come to hate. The light was still on in the living room. Through the curtains she could see her father pacing back and forth. She had no idea what time it was, but she knew she was arriving home long after the curfew he had set. As she walked up the sidewalk to the front door, Katie clenched her fists. After the horrible evening with Rod, she knew that she could not cope with what her father was going to say and do. She took her key from her purse. Fearing what was ahead for her, Katie longed for the days when the easiest and best thing for her to do was to run away. Disappearing out of their lives for a while, thought Katie as she turned her key in the lock, was no longer possible. If she had learned nothing else from Mary, it was that she must take a stand and face the problem. Katie took a deep breath and entered the house knowing that perhaps tonight she would take one of the most important stands she had ever taken.

CHAPTER THIRTEEN

During the morning shift when the store was still cool, Katie wore a sweater to hide the marks on her arms. She explained the redness on her face by saying that as she boarded the bus last night, a mugger tried to grab her purse. When she yanked it away from him, the man had struck her in the face. Mr. Boswell and the other employees were sympathetic with Katie for what she had gone through. Several commented on how brave she must have been, and a few believed that in trying to defend herself from a mugger, she had risked her life. Katie smiled and tried to respond to the other workers, feeling guilty all the while about the lie that she had told them.

Marjorie was not as easily fooled. "Your old man hit you, didn't he?"

Katie felt no need to lie to Marjorie. Her friend knew all about Katie's father and mother. "He went crazy, Marjorie. I never saw him act so wild and angry."

"You shouldn't have allowed him to do it. You allowed it to happen. I'm telling you that's how my ex did me. I just stood there and let him do it. I was as sick as he was. You just can't let them do it to you."

Katie fought to keep the tears from falling. "Do you think I let him do this? Is that what you think?"

"Why didn't you run or something? Pick up a lamp and bop him. Anything. Just look at your face. I bet he got you other places."

"My arms. They're a mess. Marjorie, I swear when I

170

walked into that house I knew he was going to be fuming. I figured I was going to take a stand against him, and I wasn't going to let him touch me ever again. It happened so fast. Just so darn fast."

Marjorie eased up on her judgment of Katie. "Okay, kiddo. I'm sorry for what I said. I know it isn't always that easy. I'm just talking out of turn."

"He grabbed me when I went in the door. I never had a chance against him. He just started swinging and hitting and calling me names. Oh, darn, Marjorie, I hate it so much when he starts that name calling about me being a tramp and having Michael. He's just cruel. Just a horrible, cruel man."

"What did your mom do?"

"The same thing she always does. She calls out, 'Now, Bob, don't be too hard on Katie.' For crying out loud he's belting me around and that crazy woman is telling him not to be too hard on me. She is sick, Marjorie. Real sick. Mary says my mother can't help it and she won't change if she doesn't get some help. I don't know if she could ever get enough help to make her change. She's so used to living the way we live, she doesn't know anything different."

Marjorie glanced at her watch. "Hey, listen, our break is over. I think this is the end for you, Katie. You got to get out of there. After work I'm going to show you this place I found. It's only got one bedroom, but it's got this little alcove that we can use for Todd. I think between the two of us we can afford one of those sofa things that opens up into a bed. You just got to get out of that place. You're going through a living nightmare." Marjorie wrapped her arm around Katie's shoulder and gave her a squeeze. "Hang tough, kid. We're going to work this out."

All day Katie's arm ached as she pulled the groceries from the cart and slid them across the computer that rang up the prices. Four o'clock and the end of her working day seemed a long way off no matter when she looked at the clock. When her shift was over, Katie was drained not only from what her father had done to her, but from staying awake all night. She lay awake through the night not only from the physical pain that she felt, but from the aching sadness that would not leave her because of Rod.

After work Marjorie pulled her car around to the front of the store and Katie slid onto the front seat. "Everything, I mean everything, aches." Katie dropped her head against the seat. "I don't know if I have enough energy to look at an apartment."

Her friend reached over and slapped Katie's knee. "You got to get with it, Katie. You'll get excited when you see the place. The landlord just painted it. It's all bright looking. Hey," Marjorie nibbled on a candy bar as she pulled out into the street, "you like plants?"

"I guess. I never had any."

"I bet you anything that you'll like them. It's pretty neat watching things grow. I got about eight plants. You can help me keep them watered." Marjorie wasn't sure if

172

she should keep talking in an effort to get Katie's mind off her problems, or if she should remain silent and let her rest. She chose to the do the latter thing. "Just lay there and rest, kiddo. It's only about fifteen minutes from here. The neighborhood leaves a lot to be desired, if you know what I mean, but the inside of the place is pretty nice. Did I tell you that the landlord has got it all newly painted?"

Katie nodded and closed her eyes. She wished she could feel some excitement about going to look at the apartment, but she simply was too tired. "Can we afford it?" Katie rolled her head toward Marjorie.

"It's not all that fancy, Katie Just a real ordinary three rooms. The important thing is that we get you away from that lunatic old man of yours."

Katie winced at the thought of him and what he had done to her. "I really don't know how I'm going to get out of that place. He'll stop me. I know he will."

"And why don't you just get yourself to the police and tell them what he does to you? They'll lock him up."

"It's my word against his."

"Your word *and* those bruises. If he were my old man, I'd see that he got locked up for the rest of his life."

"I don't think it works that way." Katie felt more weary by the minute.

"This is it." Marjorie stopped in front of a four-story brick building. "Up and up and away we go. It's on the fourth floor and there's no elevator. That's why it's cheap and would only attract the young and healthy. Ready?"

173

Katie pulled on the door handle and slid out of the car. By the time they reached the last flight of stairs, Katie and Marjorie were panting. "They ought to rent these stairs out as a health club." Katie pressed her hand against her throat. "Golly. How's Todd going to manage this?"

"He's a tough kid." Marjorie took out the envelope that held the key to the apartment. "Stanley gave me the key. He's the landlord. Stanley's about one hundred and twelve. I don't see how he gets up here and paints. He says he's from the old country where people learn to work hard until the day they die." Marjorie pushed open the door. "So. What do you think?"

Katie looked at the sun streaming through the windows. The walls were clean and bright as Marjorie had said. "It's nice. Really nice."

"Come on and look at the bathroom. It's nothing special, but everything works." Marjorie ran the water in the sink. "I think these fixtures are the same age as Stanley, but it's clean, huh."

For the first time since Katie had left work she began to feel some excitement. "The living room is plenty big. Big enough for that sleeper we talked about getting. Maybe something in dark blue or green."

"Now you sound like the Katie I know. You got some pep in your voice."

"Do you want to know why?"

"Why?" Marjorie cracked open a window above the sink. "Some view. That is if you happen to think brick

174

makes for a great view. So what were you saying?"

"When I was in the living room I could see myself here. All I could think about was walking through a door and not having to listen to my nutty family, and not having to face my father. Oh, God, that would be wonderful!"

"Then go for it." Marjorie led the way out of the apartment. We can move in any time. Stanley doesn't have any of those lease regulations about moving in at the first of the month. He says if I want the place, it's mine." She turned the key and knocked on the door. "Home sweet home."

"How should I handle it? I mean moving out."

"You pack your stuff and say '*adios daddy*,' and then walk out."

"Marjorie, I'm only seventeen. He can make me stay."

"Darn it, Katie. Fight him. Don't let him threaten you. Stand up against him. You got rights. One of those rights is you don't have to let anyone thump on you. Tell him that."

Marjorie's words gave Katie courage, yet, she knew that when the time came to face her father, it would not be as easy as Marjorie made it sound. "I know you're right. I'll deal with it somehow." Katie took her place beside Marjorie in the car. "I didn't even tell you about me and Rod having this god-awful fight."

"Is that why you're so punky sounding?"

"Partly. He said he didn't want to kiss me or get messed up with me because I might get pregnant."

"Sounds sensible to me. You don't want to go through that again. You've already been through enough."

What Marjorie said sounded almost like what Rod had said, yet she didn't upset her the way Rod had upset her. "He was sort of saying that maybe I wasn't such a good person. Not really a tramp or anything. Just his words, Marjorie. There was something about them that hurt me."

"From what I know of Rod, I can't imagine him calling you anything like a tramp. You probably weren't paying attention to what he was saying. I think he's a nice kid from what I've seen of him."

"He is nice." Katie agreed with her. "I just wish he loved me."

"When I was a kid my mom used to tell me to be careful about what I wished for because the wish might come true."

"Nothing would make me happier than if my wish about Rod came true."

"Katie, you got the rest of your life ahead of you. Now why do you want to get yourself seriously involved with someone? Come on, give yourself a break."

"What's wrong with wanting someone to love me? Everyone wants to be loved."

"So who's arguing?" Marjorie reached for a piece of chewing gum.

"Then why do you rattle on about that stuff? Not getting seriously involved. Baloney. How can two people love each other and not get involved? You're talking

176

rubbish."

"Well, *excuse me.*" Marjorie looked at Katie. "Look at all you got to worry about, kiddo. Settling this stuff with your father. Getting yourself moved. Putting up with Todd and me. You're going to have to do some adjusting. We all are. Why do you want to take on one more problem?"

"What problem?"

"Falling in love."

"I'm already in love." Katie bit her lip to keep from crying. Again, so much of what Marjorie said sounded like another version of what Rod had said. "He just won't tell me that he loves me."

"Give him some time. He's just a kid like yourself. He's trying to grow up like any guy his age. I'll bet you anything he's confused."

"That's what he says."

"At least he's honest. Listen, Katie, you can't expect all that much out of him. Every time you talk about him you tell me about some nice thing that he's done. You see each other now and then, and you have some good times together. Why do you want to turn the whole thing into a big production? Go with what you got. You'll have the rest of your life to fall head over heels in love. Like I said, give the guy a break."

"Then you don't think he meant it when he said that stuff about..." Katie couldn't even remember exactly what he had said that made her feel so terrible.

"Said what?"

177

"I can't remember," Katie laughed. "I honestly can't remember. All I know is that he hurt my feelings."

Marjorie stopped the car about a block from where Katie lived. "Hey, kiddo, I know that guy didn't mean to hurt your feelings. He was probably just trying to tell you how he honestly felt. I'll bet you anything you jumped all over his case."

In thinking back over what had happened, Katie felt sad in knowing that what Marjorie said was true. "I suppose I did. Now he's really going to think I'm a stupid jerky fool."

"They got prisons and erasers for people who make big mistakes. For people like you, we got the word *sorry*. Tell him you're sorry you blew your cork. And, ease up on him. Just go out with him and enjoy his company and see what happens. Don't be laying all that pressure on him. You might think he's all grown up, but Rod is just a kid. He's probably not any more sure what to do than you are."

"I think I'm doing what Mary warned me about."

"That Mary. She's always got a warning or a word of wisdom. What did she warn you about this time?"

"Oh, she doesn't know about me and Rod fighting."

"I expect she will." Marjorie grinned and turned off the engine. "So what was the warning?"

"That I'm looking for love and affection, and that I'm probably trying to make Rod responsible for giving them to me. That's not fair, is it?"

"It doesn't even come close to fair. There's no way that

kid can make up for your rotten dad. You got to get your own life in order. At least you quit so much of that running yourself down baloney. Now just go with the flow and don't be expecting Rod to love you and make up for your mom and dad. Okay?" Marjorie turned the key in the ignition. "I got to go get Todd. His babysitter probably thinks I disappeared off the face of the earth. You going to be okay now?"

"Thanks, Marjorie."

"For what?"

"For being my friend."

"It's my pleasure." She tapped Katie's arm, and Katie winced. "Oh, sorry about that. Are you going to do battle tonight?"

"When are you moving in?"

"Say the word."

"This weekend."

Marjorie blew out a puff of air. "That was a mighty quick word. I have to think a minute. Maybe I can get my brother and his wife to help us. I'm going to need some muscle to get my couch and bed out of my place. Can I call and let you know?"

"No. Don't call. Let me know at work tomorrow. As soon as you tell me you got someone to help, I'll tell them I'm leaving. You'll be able to hear the explosion all over town. It's a scary thought."

"As soon as I know anything, I'll let you know. Remember, hang tough. You got me and Mary. And you got that Rod if you'd give him half a chance."

"I know." Katie gave Marjorie a kiss on the cheek. "Having you three is three more than I ever had in my life."

Katie walked the block to her house. She wondered how many more times she would follow the sidewalk that led to the house where people never could talk to each other. As she neared her house, she wondered if she would walk there a few more times or if she would walk there until she was eighteen and free to leave.

CHAPTER FOURTEEN

It was late into the week before Marjorie let Katie know that it would be two weeks before she could get the help that she needed to move. In the meantime Katie told Mary of her plans.

Looking at Katie's facial welt that was only now beginning to fade, Mary didn't argue with Katie about her moving out of her parents' house, nor did she try to point out the problems that Katie would face trying to support herself. Now Mary had come to realize that the best thing for Katie to do was to get away from her parents.

"You know you can count on me and Donald to help you. His uncle has a truck. Why between Marjorie's family and us, we can have all your things and all Marjorie's things moved into the apartment in less than a day. Are you excited, Katie?"

"Right now I'm more afraid than excited. I just never really thought the day would come when I'd have to face them down."

"They should have been faced a long time ago." Mary poured Katie a soda. "I'm not blaming you, girl. You were just too young and you didn't know how to deal with it. I just wish the people at your school had gotten themselves involved more. It's a problem, though. The teachers never know just how far they can go when it comes to interfering in the life of one of their students. Lord knows, though, how many times you must have come to school with bruises and welts on you."

Mary sat down and stroked Katie's hair. "It isn't that the grown ups don't want to help you children. It's that sometimes we don't know how to help. We don't have all the answers. We want to do the right thing, but darned if we always know what that is."

Katie thought about all the times her father had hit her or called her names. "When I was real little I used to hope and pray someone would see what he was doing and just pound him one. Then I'd get scared that maybe someone would do it. You know what's strange, Mary? Here he was hitting on me and hurting me, and yet I couldn't stand the thought of anyone hurting him. I'm this little eight-year-old kid and I want to protect my dad from getting hurt. Why didn't he feel the same way about me?"

"Because you're a sweet, lovely girl with compassion. Even at eight you knew it was wrong to hit people. You knew in your heart that he shouldn't be whipping you, but somehow he made you think you deserved it. That's why some kids grow up so confused. They just don't know what's right. They love their parents to death. Those same parents are working them over good. Oh, Lord, the human emotions are really something."

"I'm just beginning to find that out. We got all these feelings running around inside us, but we don't understand them. Maybe I'm starting to understand how some of them got in my head. That's about as tough to deal with as ignoring them."

"Now, child, don't you ever ignore feelings. They're
182

there for a reason. They're like a message. You pay
attention to your feelings and don't bury them. So what
time do you want us at your place on Saturday?"

"With no more than what I got to take along, you can
just drive past and I can pitch my suitcase in the car. You
better go to Marjorie's first."

"Are you going to delay it until the last minute?"

"What?"

"Don't you look at me like that, little girl. You know
darn well what I'm talking about. In fact, I think we ought
to be there when you tell your parents what you're going to
do. I'm concerned with for your safety, Katie."

"I won't let him get me this time. No more surprises
for me."

Katie chose to wait until Friday after supper before
telling her parents that she was leaving. The only protection Katie sought was to ask Bobbie to be present when she
gave them the news. Despite his being nervous about her
request, Bobbie did as she asked him to do. Watching for
her signal, Bobbie waited in the kitchen until Katie began
speaking. Then he came and sat down in the living room.
If his father went after Katie, Bobbie was not sure what he
could do to protect her. Like all of the children, Bobbie did
not respect his father. He only feared him. What Katie was
going to do not only astounded Bobbie, but it made him
feel some sense of pride in his sister. He thought of her
defiance as an act of bravery. He would like to do the same
thing, but he questioned whether he could ever get up the

courage to defy his father.

Katie sat across from her father. She knew that he had no way of knowing that she had packed all her things. Behind her closed bedroom door were the boxes and suitcase that contained everything she owned. Though she had said nothing to her sisters about her moving out, they noticed that Katie's belongings were gone from the drawers and shelves, and that Katie would be leaving once again. They seemed to sense that what was going to happen this time between Katie and her parents was going to be a very serious quarrel. None of her sisters spoke a word about the packed suitcase and wrapped cartons hidden in the bedroom.

Katie had hoped her father would set his paper aside as he sometimes did to rest his eyes. When he didn't, she asked, "Could you stop reading the paper for a minute, Dad?" Katie stared across at him. She folded her hands to keep them from trembling.

"No, I can't." He turned the page and once again hid his face behind the newspaper.

"I'm leaving, dad. I got everything ready to go."

He dropped the paper into his lap. "What are you talking about? Lucy. Lucy, get in here. This crazy kid of yours is off and running again."

Lucy appeared in the doorway. "What's the problem now?"

"Tell your mother what you just said."

The level of Katie's voice rose. "I'm leaving."

"Leaving for what? What are you talking about?" Lucy wiped her hands on her apron.

"Leaving for good. Leaving forever and all time."

"Well, I got news for you." Katie's father rose out of the chair. "You're not going any place until I put you out. I'm the one running this house and you'll do what I tell you."

"Not anymore I won't." Katie answered him defiantly.

Bobbie cringed at the words Katie spoke to her father. "Easy, Katie. Calm down." Bobbie could see his father coming after her in one of his rages. He not only feared for Katie, he feared that in the end he would be a coward and not help his sister.

"Have you taken leave of your senses or what?" He moved closer to her.

"Don't you dare touch me!" Katie rose up and moved away. Her cat-like movements and her ability to dodge him to stay out of his reach were something at which she had a great deal of practice. There were hundreds of times when she had tried to scoot away from him, or had tried to protect herself by putting furniture between herself and the father who wanted to punish her.

"Since when did you start giving the orders around here?" His face had long since turned red with anger.

"I'm not giving any orders. I'm stating a fact. You are not going to hit me ever again. And I'm leaving."

"Over my dead body. I'll have the law down on you so hard you'll wish you had never opened your mouth."

"I just wish I had opened my mouth, as you say, a long time ago." Katie continued to move about the room as her father kept trying to get closer to her. From time to time Katie shot a glance toward Bobbie. She could tell he was nervous and afraid. In the end, Katie knew that he would not help her. Her break for her own freedom and a chance at doing something with her life now depended on what she did and said.

"You can send the police after me if you want, but I won't come back here. I want a normal life, and as long as you and mom act so crazy and do so many cruel things to me, I can't have a normal life. I'm tired of being afraid. Afraid of what you're going to say to me. Afraid that you're going to hit me."

Lucy spoke up. "That's nonsense, Katie. None of the other children are afraid of us. Why what kind of parents would we be if our children were afraid of us?"

"We're all afraid. It's just I'm the only one who tells the truth." She wanted to yell at them to look at Bobbie hunched over and terrified that his father would turn on him. Katie decided it was pointless to use Bobbie as an example in her own struggle against her parents.

Bob Bennett threw the newspaper on the floor. "You won't be smarting off so much at the mouth when the police come after you."

"And when they do, I'm going to tell them about you and how you hit on me. How you've been hitting me for years. How you insult me and try to make me feel all rotten about myself. Do you think the police would like to hear that?"

"It's your word against the word of me and your mother. Just look around here at what a nice place we got. Now you don't suppose any policeman is going to believe that we pick on you. Why this house is spotless."

Katie shook her head at his lack of reasoning. "What does having a clean house have to do with you hitting me? Are you trying to say that only kids who live in dirty houses get hit? That's what I mean about this crazy place. You don't even think right. You just invent some idea because it sounds good. Well, those ideas don't sound so good to me anymore. They sound nuts."

"You're going to be nuts, young lady, when they lock you up and throw away the key." His temple throbbed and he felt pains in his chest because of his rage with Katie.

"I got proof of what you've done, dad. I've worn all the bruises I'm ever going to wear. My teachers know about you. Mary knows what you've done to me. Sister Loretta will come to court for me. How about that? A nun telling the judge that it's true that you whip me. Now who do you think the judge will believe?"

"Stop it!" Bob Bennett screamed at her. "You just shut that nasty mouth of yours."

"I don't have a nasty mouth. I have a truthful mouth. The truth is I'm leaving. And the truth is if you try to stop me, I'm going to get all my teachers and friends to come to court. You're the one they'll lock up, and I'll just bet they'll throw away the key."

Katie turned and ran from the room. This time she was not crying. She felt strong and good about what she had said and what she was about to do. Just to make sure that she was safe through the night, Katie pulled the dresser over against the door so that she could hear her father coming if he tried to enter her room. Her sisters sat and watched her struggling with the dresser. Finally Betsy stood up to help her.

"Are you really leaving for good, Katie?"

"That I am. If he starts hitting on you after I leave, you let me know. We'll all do something about it"

Betsy pulled her robe tighter. "Not me. I'm not getting dad in any trouble."

"Maybe you'll learn like I had to learn."

"You don't love dad that's your problem."

Katie leaned against the wall and thought about what Betsy said. "Maybe you're wrong, Betsy. I probably do love him and mom. I just don't like what they do. I suppose a kid can't help loving her parents, but that doesn't mean I have to put up with them hurting me."

"Are you ever going to come and see us?"

"You can come and see me."

"What about mom and dad? Aren't you ever going to come and see them?"

"Later maybe. I got to wait until I don't feel so much pain. Maybe when we can be nice to each other if that day ever gets here."

"Are you sad about leaving?"

"What kind of question is that? Of course, I'm sad." Katie scooted in the bed beside Melba. "This is the only home I've ever had. Why wouldn't I be sad?"

Melba pulled at a strand of hair. "If you're sad, then why do you have to go?"

"Because that's my decision." Katie lay back on the bed and held Melba tightly to her. "I'll miss you all. Melba, I want you to know that I love you." Katie kissed her younger sister. "I really love you all."

"Don't go, Katie." Melba put her arm across Katie's stomach.

"Yeah," Betsy added. "You don't have to decide tonight what to do."

"Oh, Betsy, I decided a long time ago what to do. It's like I made this final decision about what would be best for me. Staying here is not what's best for me."

Katie reached over and turned off the light. Tears fell down her face at knowing this would be the last time she would ever sleep in her bed and lay beside Melba. Katie brushed the hair from Melba's forehead. "You just always remember that no matter what happens here, I love you and you can always come to me for help."

Melba moaned softly and fell off to sleep in Katie's arms. As Katie lay looking at the moon shining through the bedroom window she wished that when she had been Melba's age that someone would have told her she was loved and that someone would always be there to help her.

In the morning the ringing of the doorbell was ignored. Bob and Lucy Bennett knew the sound of the bell meant that someone had come to help Katie carry out her plan. Katie walked through the living room to open the door. At the sight of Donald, she smiled.

"I'll get my suitcase, but I'll need some help carrying my boxes of stuff."

Bobbie jumped up. "I'll help you, Katie."

Mr. Bennett dug his fingers into Bobbie's shoulder. "Sit right where you're at. There isn't anyone in this house that's going to do one single thing to help this girl get herself in more trouble."

Bobbie dropped back into the chair and watched Donald and Mary tote Katie's boxes to the car. When all her things were packed in the trunk, Katie turned to Bobbie. "Will you give me a hug and kiss goodbye?"

Something in him made Bobbie want to do as she asked, but the strangeness of hugging and kissing his sister caused him to shake his head. "Bye, Katie. Take it easy, okay."

"That I'll do." Katie turned to her mother. "I know hugs and kisses aren't any big deal around here, but would you kiss me goodbye, mom?"

Lucy's lip trembled and she twisted her fingers "I don't think so."

Bob Bennett stood up and walked out of the room. "Don't you dare put such a question to me."

Katie looked around at the family that would always be

hers. She felt an overwhelming sense of sadness and pity. Neither the sadness nor the pity was for herself. It was for them. She turned to Mary and said, "I'm ready." Katie could barely bring forth a smile as she looked at Mary and Donald.

Once in the car, Katie looked back several times at the house. "I guess I feel like I moved forward today. Do you think I did, Mary?"

"You been moving forward, sweetie, ever since I met you."

"I somehow think I could come back here a hundred years from now and things would be just the same."

Donald headed toward the apartment that Katie would share with Marjorie. "Now why do I think you're exactly right."

Mary tapped him on the thigh. "Look at the brighter side. There's hope for everyone. Maybe by Katie leaving, they'll get some sense in their heads. That little Melba shows some promise. My word, but she's a spunky little girl."

"Being spunky can get you in a whole lot of trouble with that bunch. Ask me what it was like to be spunky." Katie let out a deep sigh. Relief that the ordeal was over was beginning to settle in. "I'm going to look out for her, though."

The boxes were slowly carried to the third floor. Exhausted and panting, Donald finally gave up and waited downstairs. The task of carrying boxes and furniture was left to Marjorie's young brother and to Rod who had come to help. By six that night everything that Katie and Marjorie owned had been hauled into the small apartment. The floor was covered with half opened cartons and the newspapers in which Marjorie had wrapped her breakable things.

Marjorie drew her arm across her forehead to wipe away the perspiration. "What a mess! I don't know about the rest of you, but I'm about ready to call it quits." Marjorie leaned against the wall. "I don't know if I got it in me, but I got to go get Todd. If you don't mind, Katie, I'm going to spend the night at the sitter's. If I bring Todd back here with this mess, he'll be into every carton. I don't think I can deal with that tonight."

"That's okay, Marjorie. I found some sheets and the pillows are over there." As Katie pointed to the pillows, they fell off a stack of boxes. "What luck. They fell exactly where I'm going to sleep."

Mary looked as tired as the rest of them. "I better get downstairs and get Donald poured into the car." Mary laughed. "That man is just beginning to realize that this thing called age is creeping up on him." Mary gave Katie a hug and a kiss. "You better call it quits yourself, child. You've already done a mountain of work today. Will you call me in the morning?"

"We won't have a phone until next week."

"Well, I can't wait until next week to find out how you're doing. You get yourself to a pay phone and let me know how your first night as a free woman went."

"Free woman. You're crazy, Mary." Katie walked her to the door. "Look. We got our names on the door. Ms. *Katie Bennett.* How about that?"

"You're something else, sweetie. Bye for now."

"Bye, Mary."

"Hold on." Marjorie called out. "I'm right behind you. Keep the home fires burning, Katie. I'll be back early."

Katie closed the door behind them. Then she turned to Rod. "I sure want to thank you. You were a really big help. You sure can't get away from the fact that guys can carry heavier stuff than girls." She burst out laughing. "I thought you and Marjorie's brother were going to blow up by the time you got that couch of hers to the third floor. You should have seen your faces. All red and puffy."

"I just hope that neither one of you is planning on moving soon. If you want my help, I think I'd just dump the couch and the bed out the window straight into a moving van. Are you hungry?"

Katie leaned her back against the wall and slid to the floor. "Yeah. I really am, but I have to rest for a few minutes." Katie glanced around at all that still had to be done. "I really ought to wash up before we go." She leaned her head down and sniffed. "Whew! I stink."

"Me, too." Rod dropped down on the floor beside Katie. ""Let's just go get some pizza or something like that. It won't matter if we smell. The pepperoni will have a stronger smell than our arm pits."

"Garlic and onion soup wouldn't help wipe out your armpit smell."

"That bad, huh."

"Pretty bad." Katie smiled at him. "Can we talk a minute?"

Without thinking, Rod drew a little away from Katie. He did not want to go through another night like the last one they had together. "Don't you think we ought to wait until we got a full stomach?"

"Eating a pizza is not going to change what I have to say."

Rod nervously rolled his tongue along the bottom of his lips. "Then I guess you better say what you got to say."

"To start with, I'm sorry."

"For what?"

"For acting so stu..." She stopped herself from saying the word *stupid*. "I started to say *stupid*. I'm not going to say that word ever again. I've heard it all my life. They nearly made me believe I was stupid, but I'm not. I made some decisions that weren't too good for me, but I'm not stupid."

"I sure never said you were."

She noticed how Rod was so in the habit of trying to defend himself against her, that he almost always said that he had not done the things that her parents had done to her.

"I know you haven't ever said that. I'm never again going to judge you because of what they've done. That's what I was doing, wasn't I?"

194

"Kind of. You sort of sometimes said things that made me believe that you thought I was going to treat you like they treated you. You never seemed to want to believe I wouldn't do those things."

"I believe it now." Katie reached over and took his hand. "You know I used to look for magic."

"Magic what?"

"Like when I'd run away. I was always deciding to run away. I was just sure that while I was gone that some kind of magic would have come to my house." Katie tilted her head upward and looked at the ceiling. "In this magic world of mine I'd be coming up the walk to my house. When I opened the door, my mom would throw her arms around me and tell me how much she loved me and missed me and worried about me. None of that ever happened. There wasn't any magic that changed her. In that nutty, magic world of mine, my dad would ask me about school. He'd come to my basketball games. And, Rod, he never hit me when I thought about my magic. Then when I'd really come home, there was the yelling and the hitting. So I decided maybe it would take longer for magic to work. I'd stay away longer and longer. No matter how long I stayed away, nothing changed."

"What about magic now?"

"I have tons of hope, Rod, but I sure don't believe in any magic or that I can live in some kind of pretend world. Oh, Rod, how I used to pretend. I'd listen to some of the kids talking at school about their moms or dads, and I swear, I'd go eat my lunch or sit in class and pretend that their parents were my parents."

"I think lots of kids do that. They always think that someone's parents are better than their own."

"You don't."

"I got a real prize for a mother. No, I sure wouldn't want anyone else to be my mother."

"Well, I can't pretend my parents aren't my parents. You know, Rod, that's why I think I'm more grown up than they are. I accept them for who they are. They'd never do that with me. I sort of figured out these last couple of months that they probably won't change. I could win the Miss America contest and they'd call the judges to tell them they made a mistake. It's me, Rod, who's got to change."

"I'm telling you, Katie, it's going to be all right. Everything is going to work out."

"No, Rod, things don't just work out. You got to *make* them work out. You got to do something to help yourself. I have to start thinking things through, and when I make a decision, it's got to be a good one."

"Moving in with Marjorie was a good one. I can tell you that." He felt safer putting his arm around Katie. "You know I think you're one of the most grown up girls that I've ever met."

"So!" She rubbed his nose with her finger. "There are other women in your life!"

"Well, let's see. There's Tiffany and Amber. I see

them on the weekend. Then there's Sara and Sandy and Sally. My mind is just going blank and I can't think of all their names."

"Yeah, I bet." Katie grinned and stood up. "You just be thinking about how you're going to pay for your pizza instead of worrying about all these women in your life."

"I thought you were paying."

"You're wrong. I paid last time, and then you insulted me on top of that."

Rod blushed at her reminding him of the night she had raced to the bus without even saying goodbye. "That was a bad news night."

Katie's fingers brushed his cheek. "It was my fault. I just got a lot of growing up to do. Not as much as you do, of course," she teased, "but enough."

"Are you sure you don't want me to move these cartons into the kitchen before we leave?"

"Come on, Rod. You've done enough. Me and Marjorie will get them in the morning." Katie picked up the key and kissed it. "Just one more thing, Rod, before we go stuff our faces. I want you to know that I don't hold you responsible for making me happy."

"Hey, listen, I know that." He said the words, but he really felt that she did want him to make her happy.

"Liar. Liar." Katie sort of sang the words and smiled. "Remember you said that we had to be honest with each other. I'm being honest now. I know that you and no one else can make me feel good about myself. I have to do that on my own. I'm just going to look at the things I do and I'm going to tell myself that they are pretty good things." Katie leaned against him. "I really love you, Rod. It doesn't matter whether you feel that way about me or not. I love you for all the help you've been to me. I love you for being there when I needed you. Those are important reasons to love someone. I just want you to know that you can't make up for my rotten parents."

"I do care about you, Katie."

He still didn't use the word *love*.

"Then that's good enough for me for now. Besides, I'm too busy to worry all that much about love. By the time I get all those cartons unpacked, I'll be so exhausted I might sleep the rest of my life."

"Yeah. I got a picture of that. You got the key?"

She waved it in the air and grinned. "I'm for real, Rod. I got so much of my life that I got to get straightened out. No more magic. Everything isn't going to be all right in the morning. It's going to take a long time to get my act together."

"Oh, I kind of like the act you got going now." He pulled the door closed and looked at her fingers turning the key.

"If you think this act is something, you hang tough, as Marjorie says, and see what's coming."

Rod followed her down the flight of stairs. "I still think you ought to pay."

Katie smiled to herself and said, "I'm done paying,

Rod. Now I'm going to start living and getting it together."

Rod thumped Katie gently on the head as he raced her down the stairs. "I'm behind you one hundred percent."

"You know who else is behind what I do?"

"Who?"

"Me."